ARTISTS
IN SAN MIGUEL
AND OTHER STORIES

FRANCISCO JAVIER MORALES ERCAMBRACK

historiasjm@yahoo.com

CONTENTS

To Ana, Laura, and my parents' memory

ARTISTS IN SAN MIGUEL

I

LOVE AT FIRST SIGHT

Luciano cleared his throat. He knew he had to be in tune from the start of the song. Bono paid attention to all the movements of his companion. He gave the impression that he would limit himself to being only the accompanying voice. Not too many seconds passed when Bono became tense, awaiting the problems that were about to begin. Then, both turned their heads to allow their eyes to meet. This was about a casual meeting, like the one we experience when we pass through any place. However, anyone attentive to body language could guess that a discreet but intense spark of hate came out from their eyes, like those that appear when two rocks collide intentionally, with violence.

They were both nervous, despite being a pair of professional singers. Perhaps this was not a voice duel, but a stingy competition of egos. Who could sing better? Bono or Luciano? Luciano would shine as usual with a song where a deep voice was needed to go up and down masterfully, so the diners would feel that the scenario boomed with exquisite harmony.

If Bono's voice was more modest, he did have the necessary mastery to almost hypnotize those present and make them dance or sing. However, if a modern song inspired him, Luciano will have problems. How was it possible for Bono to take over the performance and not Luciano? For God's sake! Nature is wise due to something, and not everyone was granted the same vocal cords. In addition, here in San Miguel at the restaurant-bakery La Buena Vida, the famous and acclaimed artist is Luciano. Not the mimicking Irish singer who, according to those who know what they say, has neither a foreign passport nor was born in Europe.

Luciano has thought that it is more probable that Bono was born someplace close to Queretaro or Atotonilco rather than outside the country. But, like he would say, in this world and all the others that may have existed, facts are facts, and the idle talk and envies are like boiling saliva that makes the mouths of gossipers and jealous people boil. "Poor inferior beings," Bono said on one occasion in which he and Luciano were still friends and sang old Beatles songs in chorus. "If they don't spit it out and hurt their neighbors, they will be poisoned by all the venom they have in their bodies"—so ended Bono the phrase with a deep breath. At that time, Luciano and Bono would sing Beatles songs with gusto. Those were times of friendship, camaraderie, and happiness.

Luciano was aware of speculation regarding Bono and the gossip and the gossipmongers. Therefore, he pretended when it was necessary to act. Because of this, even though Bono was not totally to his liking these days, Luciano treated him with respect, recalling the old friendship between them because he was an honorable gentleman who didn't mistreat anyone. He also knew that in show business, one cannot talk bad about others, not because of karma or costly lawsuits for slander, but because in this environment, everything that is said today returns tomorrow like a sharp boomerang to cut out the tongue and throat of the gossiper. "Ooof, better not open my beak," thought Luciano.

For a moment, there was a convenient silence. Luciano and Bono, not wanting, took a deep breath, as if they were sighing. Who knows what they recalled, or what feelings were harbored in their hoarse chests? If Luciano had had a powerful microphone in his reach, he would have made the stones of all the churches vibrate around there and conquered the ears of all the diners at Tio Lucas, the Finestra Cafe, the Cafe de Bellas Artes, and all the other places in the area. For example, those at the Tio Lucas would have stopped eating the succulent meat dishes and ask the jazz group that played there to remain silent, while Luciano enchanted their ears with his splendid voice.

Those who know a lot about art, and more about artists, say that the rivalry, so as not to say hate, between Luciano and Bono began that time when an elegant and attractive woman arrived at La Buena Vida. Lady Beautiful, they called her. She had a lovely hairdo with yellow feathers, and she stared at both artists attentively. She distracted Luciano and Bono and made them make mistakes in their songs. It seemed that she had stolen their souls and the movement in their vocal cords.

From the moment Lady Beautiful arrived at to La Buena Vida, the rivalry between the singers started. They began to hate each other. Finally, Luciano changed his attitude, and when Bono sang, it was coincidental that his throat was hoarse with a lot of r's, as if something was caught in his vocal cords. Bono began to cough loudly, as if he had the flu. There was one occasion when he did this in a vulgar manner, for which even he was embarrassed.

Oh! A beautiful friendship that went berserk and was lost just because a lovely lady came one day and flirted with both famous artists at the same time. The problem did not end then. That heart thief separated friends and made them jealous of one another. For example, there was that day when she arrived at La Buena Vida and went to a high part of that place. From there she looked at Bono fixedly. He went mute with emotion. He became distracted and began to draw the attention of the beautiful, unknown lady. As of that moment, he included in his repertoire some romantic songs like "Strangers in the Night," "Come to Me," and "Never, My Love." Not even Frank Sinatra, the Bee Gees, or the Association could have sung them with so much feeling and love as Bono did.

II

THE BOLERO BY RAVEL

Luciano realized that Bono had fallen in love with Lady Beautiful. He did not say one word; he did not even open his mouth. He feigned not noticing and kept silent. The next time Lady Beautiful appeared at La Buena Vida, everything happened fast, as if she had arrived flying at great speed. Once again, she went to the high part of the place. Now, it was Luciano who felt an uncontrollable impulse. He breathed deeply but did not clear his throat. Then, in a wink, he began to hum "Bolero," by Ravel. He started softly, but with a powerful and sure voice that went high into the sky. As he increased the energy of the musical piece, he did the same with the melodious sound and the profound emotion that came out of his mighty throat. His voice was that of the lover who is showing irrepressible joy and is about to go mad because the loved one is near. He didn't know it, but his legs were moving without his knowledge and taking him where the charming and maddening lady awaited him. "Bolero" is the excuse to start the trek to the sky. The lover's emotion increases when he sees his loved one has extended her hand for him to take. He feels that her hand burns in his, and he takes it to his lips and kisses it passionately. This is a moment of total exaltation, strength, emotion, and ecstasy that Luciano transmits through the musical piece he is humming. The sounds emanating from his throat join a perfect sequence of movement, passion, and force. The artist, through love, has conquered all. He can extend his wings and know he is the owner of the world, perfection, the best voice that exists, and the love of the loved one. He does not ask for more, nor is there any more.

The whole world remained openmouthed by Luciano's performance. Bono could not hide his admiration. According to San Miguel's inhabitants, inside the Church of St. Michael, a few blocks away, Luciano's humming of "Bolero" was heard with great passion and energy. Those inside the church listened enraptured to the master and watched as the stones of the central aisle vibrated. The parishioners were astounded by the emotion produced by the artist's singing.

The fact that he had hummed "Bolero," by Ravel, made some of San Miguel's inhabitants think that it would be marvelous if Luciano could sing every Sunday at noon to one side of the altar of the Church of St. Michael. There, his voice would make the whole church vibrate, and his singing would be a heavenly call for angels and cherubs and young fellows to meet in that church and listen to an angelic interpretation of Bach's "Ave Maria." They would come from the St. Philip Neri Church, the Temple of the Nuns, and the San Francisco Temple. Then, all those beings would go to the midday mass, during which Luciano would sing to purify their ears and minds. They would take the memory of that singing that filled them with joy in their daily heavenly activities.

III
Rain and Wind

It was cloudy as day broke—only black clouds were seen. In San Miguel, a strong wind was blowing that swept through all the streets. One powerful gust of cold, icy wind came down through Canal Street. At the same time, another blast came from Hernandez Macias Street, slamming the doors and windows of the houses. La Buena Vida, which is on Hernandez Macias, underwent significant damage. Tables and chairs fell here and there. The wind also strongly jostled Luciano's and Bono's cages. The first one to fall was Bono's. It was his lucky day. His little home was destroyed in the fall, but nothing happened to him. The door of his small prison opened, and he came out of his wire box. He couldn't believe it. He extended his wings and was immediately pulled into an air current. He maneuvered the best way he could, and without meaning to, he was flying over La Buena Vida.

The blowing wind and the heavy rain that was just beginning pushed Bono toward the north, toward the Church of St. Michael. Then, another strong blast of wind pushed him toward Juarez Park. From afar, he saw the San Miguel Dam. He was fearful that the wind would take him there, and that he would drown. The first thing he did was go toward a large group of trees. It was El Charco del Ingenio. Inside, he felt something was telling him that Lady Beautiful lived in that neighborhood. So, he flew toward that ecological reserve. He arrived exhausted and looked for a tree where he could take refuge from the rain. The water was dripping on his neck and wings by the bucketful. He was very tired. He wasn't aware of the moment he fell asleep, clinging to a branch.

At dawn, the following day, it was a bit cold. Bono woke up. He couldn't believe that he was far from his home. Everything had happened without his wanting it to. But before anything else happened, he realized that several birds were observing him attentively.

A woodpecker, who looked like it was important, asked him, "And you, where are you from? From which house did you escape?"

Bono looked at the one speaking to him and breathed in. "I did not escape; the wind brought me," he responded sadly.

The other birds looked at each other. They couldn't believe the answer they got.

"My name is Bono, and I work…I'm sorry, I meant to say *I sing*…at La Buena Vida," he told them, slightly frightened.

"You are the famous Bono?" all the birds in the tree asked, surprised. "Wow!" they exclaimed in chorus and added, "You and Luciano are our preferred sparrows. Even here in El Charco, we have heard talk about you two and the incredible songs that you sing together," the birds said to him, enthused. Bono smiled. "It isn't that much, boys," he said, "I only do what I learned to do."

Another carpenter bird, who was on a higher branch, spoke to the swallow beside it. They seemed to agree on something, and then the swallow said, "Listen, Bono, is it true that you and Luciano distanced yourselves from each other because of Lady Wicked?"

Bono answered, "I only know a Lady Beautiful, boys."

"Bono," they said to him cautiously, "don't take this the wrong way, but Lady Beautiful is Lady Wicked."

"And why is that bad?" Bono asked.

There was a long and annoying silence. Then the woodpecker that had first spoken to Bono said in a severe voice, "She is a bad woman. She comes and goes through these places and dedicates herself to stealing hearts, destroying careers, and making friends hate each other."

Bono listened to these affirmations astounded. His beak was opened, and his thoughts were back on his memories.

"I tell you with sadness, Bono, all of this is true," the woodpecker said softly. He then added, "We know that close to the Atotonilco Church, another pair of sparrows sang marvelously. What happened? Lady Wicked arrived, and Elvis and Elton, their names, started fighting. Now they hate each other. Let no more be said. We will let you rest. And you can stay here as long as you wish. Isn't that so, boys?"

The rest of the birds agreed.

A huge group of feathered beings flew perfectly synchronized into the east from the tree where Bono was perched and from many other trees nearby. Bono was sad and thoughtful. He had been a fool. One such Wicked Lady had bewitched him. The worst of it was that he had let her deceive him. He remembered the times that Luciano had taught him to sing. He felt bad and uncomfortable with himself, knowing that from a vain illusion, he had lost a friend. "Bono," he told himself, fully convinced, "you must fix this. Think of a plan, and then follow it."

IV

FRIENDS COME TOGETHER ONCE AGAIN

Luciano was depressed. Three weeks had passed since the day of the windstorm. His cage had also fallen noisily, and he had hit his head and hurt a wing. He felt he would die. Little by little, however, he recovered consciousness. The blurred vision gradually cleared. He saw that Bono's cage was on the ground, destroyed. He was fearful when he didn't hear him. "Bono, my friend, you must be dead like I almost was. Please forgive me. I was a fool. I allowed myself to be deceived by a pretty face," Luciano told himself with profound sadness.

Some weeks later, the noise came little by little. It was coming from the east and seemed like an unceasing and out-of-tune prattle, much like the one musicians in an orchestra make when they tune their instruments moments before a concert. A little while later, in San Miguel and its vicinity, a massive group of birds of all types came into view. The birds first flew over the Church of St. Michael. They went around it several times. Finally, a spiral similar to that of the Milky Way appeared in the sky over the church. The birds went to greet the town's patron saint, and then they flew toward Hernandez Macias, between Canal and Mesones Streets.

Luciano continued to be pensive. He wasn't aware that, around La Buena Vida, there were thousands of woodpeckers, sparrows, ducks, white herons, doves, canaries, and other bird species. Someone seemed to coordinate everything and to say, "One, two, three, four" and immediately there was an explosion of voices. In the beginning, one could hear the ducks' *quack-quack*, the doves' *oos-oos*, and the woodpeckers' *tams-tams* the moment they hit their beaks into the trees. Then, the sparrows and canaries intervened with high and quick voices.

Luciano was surprised: he couldn't believe what he heard and saw from his cage. There was a pause. He guessed. He waited for four beats and began to sing, full of joy and enthusiasm, "With a Little Help from my Friends." During the second line, Bono's voice came together with Luciano´s voice. He flew toward the place where his cage had been. The two friends sang this song again, as they had done before, with enthusiasm and camaraderie. All the birds of San Miguel and its surroundings saw with delight how the singing of those two great artists re-established an old friendship.

The song ended. Then all the birds took flight. Luciano was happy because he knew that Bono and his friends would return. In the air, the birds began to hum, under Bono's direction, "Here Comes the Sun." Then, intuitively, they flew toward the Church of St. Michael and made several turns around it. For some, this generated an optical effect, and for others, it was a way that these birds had to say goodbye.

According to the inhabitants of San Miguel, at that moment, the Church of St. Michael was filled with light and joy.

Little Fortune Birds

I

Carrafas

Young man, don't go beyond this line; I'm working. Can't you see that your frame in this small space where I must work is distracting me a lot and is a little disturbing? I, like you, earn my living and some tiny seeds with my work efforts. So, please, I ask you to remove your hands from this plank where our owner, manager, or boss, whatever you'd like to call him, places our cage and the box that contains the little fortune cards that we pull out hastily with our beaks for the benefit of our customers. I speak in the plural because to one side of this, your humble house, is Chispita, the most beautiful female canary I know, and, on the other, Carrafas, your servant. I'll take the liberty of commenting that even though Chispita and I are confined to the same general space, we each have our own place because inside this small cage is a division that keeps us apart. In addition, each one of us has an access door to the work area. This avoids confusion about the times and sequence of our presentations of this modest, although very professional, spectacle.

I do think that, deep down, the decision to separate Chispita and me contributes to there being peace between us and allows us to minimize possible labor problems since we each have our share of air without bothering the other, and each of us is responsible for his and her activities. Furthermore, Chispita and I are a little more comfortable having the division, and we can extend our wings without bothering each other. I do not doubt that Chispita thinks likewise, that she feels that way deep down: what those of us who work arduously want at the end of the day is to have a place of our own where we can rest, recover our energy, and get rid of stress. In my opinion, life is not a lottery, as the song goes, but a fierce and agitated sea, full of pressure, which, if we are not attentive, can trap us and drown us and suck from us, little by little, our joy and love of life.

These reflections lead us to always try to go peacefully through life, although it is clear, as you know, that one doesn't always reach one's goals. There is always something: stale birdseed, a reprimand from our trainer, an ungrateful customer, or any other nonsense that ruins our day, embitters our food, and bathes us in pure stress.

When I first arrived in this trade, I didn't concentrate much. I didn't pay much attention or dedicate myself to my training because I was heedful of Chispita. When I first entered this profession, Chispita had already been in it for some time with our boss. I confess I fell in love with her only a little, just what is necessary to lose concentration on my activities and sometimes dream about the beautiful things that we would do together if we had our nest. Well, as you all know, the best remedy for the misfortune of love is time—and, of course, routine. In the early days, I would make an effort to sing (you would say to "chirp") love songs to her. Oh! You should have seen the wishful thinking with which I tuned my throat; I would straighten up my chest and take in the air so that my passionate person could sing the romantic songs never heard before. So much hope and effort for nothing! No matter how much I tried to tell her, "Chispita, here is my heart, take it!" the ingrate pretended not to see me, much less hear me. In the beginning, I thought that she didn't like the songs by Manzanero and that the famous love songs by Luis Miguel did not excite her. So, I began to practice romantic melodies by Juan Gabriel. The day I felt that I had finally mastered the song "Darling," right and left, I sang it to her. Like this, with love, softly, tenderly, with all the passion that anyone in love can have, like when a man loves a woman. From the bottom of my heart, I asked her in my song to sense my despair and loneliness and to tell me when she would see me again. I stayed there many days, between harboring hope and being sad. At first, I said nothing. Her indifference was slowly breaking my heart. At that time, the left side of my chest was causing me sharp pain, and I was beginning to need air.

Internally, and from the strongest and most painful silence of my throat, I told her to come to me. I also told her to take a piece of my heart, and that even though a grille separated us, we could give ourselves the most passionate kisses that could ever exist with our beaks. Oh my God, that was yesterday!

After many days of Chispita ignoring me, I understood that it was all a vain illusion. My chirping became bitter, and like my sad and small person, it went out of order. The pain I felt inside made my life, my work, everything become just shadows, and my activities lost their attraction, their charm. As for the vacuum that I was feeling at that moment, like a knot in my throat and chest, I thought about freeing myself from Chispita. I thought that she was a black-magic woman who, just to play with my feelings, had lit my fire, my love for her. The sadness that I was submerged in also told me that I should get out of the enormous and deep emotional pothole in which I found myself. I don't know why, but it occurred to me that, to get rid of my depression, I should be bent on doing at least some valuable and well-done things in my life that would strengthen my self-esteem. I must sadly confess that, for some days, I thought that love stank. Fortunately, some days later, I began to concentrate on my activities. I aimed to take command, to be the best little fortune bird in all of Coyoacan and its surroundings. I think I've made significant progress in this field, which I may tell you about on another occasion.

In passing, I did not seek the position of a little bird of fortune—it chose me. This profession requires a bird of small size, relatively easy to train and transport, adaptable to the changing circumstances of the work surroundings, and with a quick mind. Look at me closely. Don't I provoke sympathy? There is no room for an annoying magpie or a horrendous crow, like those that, when least expected, go and try to peck some customer's eyes out. Instead, this profession calls for someone who has a way with people, with a look somewhat tender and friendly. In my opinion, as the agile and likable canary that I am, I comply with all the requirements for taking the position of the little bird of fortune.

As you know, I come every weekend to the main square of Coyoacan to bring out the little folded papers with a message about what fortune brings. Just as it can also be verified, I am working on the church's northern side. If you are coming from Avenida Universidad, I recommend that you turn into Francisco Sosa. Go straight, slowly, enjoying the view provided by the beautiful large trees that adorn that street. When you arrive at the Centenary Garden, you're almost there. In it, you can see the famous fountain of the coyotes. Cross this garden, and you get to Plaza Hidalgo. To the far south of this, that is, to the left of the church, is where we are. My boss, Chispita, and I are delighted to attend to you with our usual weekend schedule, which is from 11:30 a.m. until it gets dark.

The work begins when our first potential customers pass by. "Fortune cards! Little fortune birds! Fortune cards!" our boss yells at those passing. People, like cats, are curious. They come near. They see Chispita and me. If my companion or I establish eye contact with a possible customer, we have made a sale of our services. Our boss will tell us then after knocking on our door with his knuckles, "Come out, Chispita (or Carrafas, as the case may be), here's some birdseed." After these basic words have been uttered, the cage door opens; he places some birdseed a couple of inches away from it. Our work is to come out and jump a couple of times. The intent is to achieve a quick and gracious entry onto the stage. We quickly take (and eat) the birdseed with our beaks. Then our boss tells us, "Ring the bell" or "Push the little car." We take a small plastic bell with our beak and throw it to one side. When he mentions the little car, which is also small and made of plastic, we push it with our heads and the upper parts of our beaks. At all times, we are attentive to what our next act will be.

For this reason, young man, I resent your taking up space and inhibiting our movement—you confound us. That is, you involuntarily make us look like clumsy little birds, instead of allowing us to present our customers with our best image.

I continue with the description of my work position and of the activity that I perform. I have already commented on what we do with the bell and the little car. To make a long story short, I will say that in our spectacle, we have, up to today, twelve toys in total with which Jwe entertain our customers, particularly the children.

All of them are made of plastic, and all are small so that Chispita and I can work comfortably and efficiently and conquer our customers' preferences. Some of these plastic figures represent famous cartoon characters, which, due to royalty questions and unpaid publicity restrictions, I am not allowed to mention by name. There is also a little car that I do not doubt is in the dreams of every city kid.

Once we finish our entrance act, or presentation to the public—as far as I understand, there is a Canadian circus of great international reputation that has copied the basic principles of our way of working— we carry on with the main part of the event, which has made us world famous. Our boss places a small box for us on the worktable, which contains many little envelopes. These are of various colors (silver, green, orange, red), and it is our responsibility to nimbly take a little envelope from the box with our beak and place it gracefully on one side. As you know, Chispita and I still don't have the certificate guaranteeing that we know how to read. That is, with some embarrassment, but with a lot of professionalism, I recognize that my companion and I are illiterate. Even though this sounds hard, it is still harder to recognize. What I want to say, if what I've said was not clear, is that my companion and I are illiterate. This guarantees that we will select your fortune envelope by chance. No one intervenes between that envelope and us; there is no black hand or invisible hand.

Once we pull the envelope out of the little box with our beaks and leave it on the worktable, we return, jumping gracefully and with agility, to the section of the cage that corresponds to us. Our boss gives the envelope to the customer and charges for our services. All the cards in the envelopes that Chispita and I pull out have been printed with professionalism by a prestigious print shop, and they contain positive messages. Can you imagine what would happen to us if, in this business, we were announcing misfortunes, tragedies, or other bad things? We would only end up driving our fine customers away and, at the end of the day, sales would drop, our scarce income would be even more insufficient to cover our costs (although I don't know what they are or how much they add up to), the business would go broke, and Chispita and I would be out on the street. Since neither she nor I can fly, and we are only physically capable of jumping a little, how could either of us earn a living without this job? How could we defend ourselves from cats or rats that wanted to eat us? We are a pair of canaries that, not being able to fly despite our beautiful wings, depend on our efforts and well-intentioned work to live in dignity.

Maybe Chispita and I will have a bit of good luck, and fortune will provide us with a better future, and we won't have to live with the uncertainty of what would happen to us if our source of income were to encounter problems. However, that possibility is remote, which comforts me and leads me to ask what the future holds for her and me. Therefore, on several occasions, I was tempted to take out the envelopes and discover our own future. I thought of this for the first time one day when our work activity was slow and our boss, in a moment of neglect, left the little box with the fortune envelopes within my reach. I kept looking at the envelopes for what seemed like an eternity, but it was only seconds. Then I felt uneasy, nervous, and cold in my wings. I was stupefied just thinking about what could happen to me if I realized this rash, although essential, act of courage. I thought that, just like any other customer, I also had the right to know what the future held for me.

The temptation to discover that information was enormous. I had to control myself because I was afraid my beak would disobey me when least expected, and without my authorization, it would bring out one of the fortune envelopes. As I mentioned, I got nervous, but my anxiety levels shot even higher when I realized that the fortune card describing my future—and that my beak would select—might be one of love. Just imagine how I would feel if I were to receive a message to this effect saying: "Even though you haven't seen it, happiness is right next to you." I could not stand it! Sadness would overwhelm me! For months, I tried to bury my feelings for Chispita in the most profound depths of my being. My sadness and frustration would be enormous if they were to reappear, uncontrolled, provoked by a card foretelling the future. Even if there are things and situations in life in which it is not necessary to know how to read, I know beforehand the contents of a heartrending love letter. My heart beats quickly from fear and, at the same time, from joy, just from thinking about all this. To avoid these inconveniences, and that my heart beats rapidly in a way I cannot control, I tell myself that nothing has happened and that nothing will happen in this scope of my life. On the other hand, to do more productive things, I know I must concentrate on my work, and that I should not dare to take out the little card of my fate to know my wretched future. As a little bird of fortune committed to his profession, I ask that you remain beyond the line to allow me to work efficiently and without the possibility of making mistakes. If I get distracted, I immediately think of love, of Chispita, and of the day she will pay attention to me and I can hug her with passion with these, my poor useless wings. Meanwhile, allow me to take a breath, to sigh, to remove from me this air of sadness, and to be able to concentrate and go on with my duties.

II

CHISPITA

Young man, please don't go. If you were so kind, I would like to tell you a couple of things so that you won't leave with a bad impression of me. I could not avoid hearing everything Carrafas said, no matter how hard he tried to be discreet. Poor thing, maybe he'd stop suffering if he knew that I also love him in the same way he loves me. No matter how much I try to hide it, I also suffer for him, but I try to be stronger and control myself. My years of life counsel me to act this way.

Before Carrafas arrived, I was in love with Speedy. He was another canary who had come into the position of the little bird of fortune. Speedy was older than I; very intelligent, swift in his actions (that's how he got his name), and an excellent life companion. We fell in love. We would get together in this cage, even if we were separated by this fine wire netting inside. We lived wing-to-wing; we always tried to be together. One day, Speedy became desperate about our sad situation. He began to try to fly inside his section of the cage. He pecked the fine wire netting that separated us. He wanted to be by my side. He hurt his beak, part of his face, and the sections of his wings that he used to push against the netting that divided us. I cried bitterly upon seeing him like that. It was very painful not to be able to do anything for him. Speedy was in a bad way for a couple of days, which fortunately were holidays. He then recovered physically, but his gaze reflected enormous sadness. He would come close to me, and we would try to act like we continued to be equally happy, like before the event that affected him. One day, without warning of any kind, Speedy was dead at daybreak.

I was disconsolate. I felt like the saddest and most forsaken of widows that ever existed. I felt that my world had ended and that there was no reason at all to continue living. My boss suspended our presentations for a few days. One day, when I felt less overwhelmed, he brought Carrafas. Like you must have guessed, he is a canary that is younger than I, full of joy and thrills. He made my life smile again. One day, he began to sing very romantic and beautiful Manzanero songs to me, as well as some old Mexican love songs, rescued, and made famous again by Luis Miguel. Oh! What melodies! What intonation! What feelings of the purest love did Carrafas transmit with his throat! Many times, I've been at the point of telling him that I also love him, that I wake up every morning only thinking about him. I don't do it because I'm scared that the same thing will happen to him that happened to Speedy. I want Carrafas to be happy, since it would be excruciating for me to see him suffer as Speedy suffered. That is why, young man, I ask you not to wrongly interpret my words. Know that I am not an ungrateful female canary with no feelings. My heart belongs to Carrafas, but I will never tell him! I don't want to see him suffer anymore. I will continue in this profession as long as possible, since this is the only way I can be close to Carrafas until death does us part. If fortune permits in the next life, our sad souls may remain together forever and be joyful with his marvelous chirping.

ERIKA

I
KIRA

It was a real surprise for my sister Lucia and me to come home from school one day and find a little ball of striped fur curled up in one corner of the kitchen.

"Don't wake her up, kids. This puppy is your surprise," Mom told us.

Lucia and I couldn't restrain our joy: right before our eyes was our first pet, sleeping.

"Her name is Kira, and she is a boxer," Mom said.

"Kira, Kira, Kira," we began to chant, Lucia, and I, without realizing it. We liked her name from the beginning. On that day, our bodies were overcome with joy, and my sister and I just wanted to keep hugging the poor animal while we petted it on the head.

"Mom, Kira is cold. She's been trembling for a while," Lucia said.

"Look, kids," Mom said, after putting her hand on our pet's neck, "this puppy is nervous and afraid of you. Better leave her alone and stop lulling her to sleep; she's getting dizzy."

Lucia and I didn't want to obey. Kira couldn't be afraid of us. I felt like telling Mom, "You're wrong. She's afraid of you and not of us." The joy of having this little ball of fur in my arms made me forget I was mad about Mom's scolding. My sister and I wanted, in short, to hug our puppy forever. We didn't fight when Lucia told me, stretching out her arms, "Okay, Arturo, now it's my turn." At that time, I behaved like an adult; I didn't run upstairs to turn on the TV. I wanted to stay looking at or hugging Kira.

While Kira was in Lucia's arms, I asked myself if my puppy would be more intelligent and courageous than Lassie, Rin Tin Tin, or any other famous TV dog. To tell the truth, at that moment I also asked myself what kind of sports Kira could play when she grew up a little. On TV, I had watched a little boy play football with his dog. Kira and I, I told myself, would even play baseball together. From the face Lucia made while she was hugging Kira, I already knew that my sister was thinking about what doll clothes would fit her so she could make the pup her lady-in-waiting.

"How would Kira look in the hat with the blue bow that Mom bought me?" Lucia asked.

"Don't be so dumb, Lucia. Don't expect the puppy to behave like a doll," I told her, annoyed and trying to keep my annoyance from her.

To our parents' surprise, we didn't fight that day. Instead, it was a day like Christmas but with no dinner or presents.

"I can't believe it, Lucy. The children haven't had a single fight today," Dad said.

The truth is, before Kira came to our house, Lucia and I would fight about everything. What I hated the most about her was that she was abusive. I couldn't tolerate that she sat in the car's front seat twice in a row. For me, that was a total encroachment on my rights and my family obligations, even though Lucia was older than I was. However, Kira's arrival brought a period of stability that consisted of a pause in our fights and discussions.

Furthermore, during the first weeks after Kira's arrival home, all our energy and activity had Kira as the only center of attraction. It would make us laugh to see her running in the garden or the kitchen, because her ears would swing from one side to the other, momentarily covering her eyes. Unfortunately, her ears were quite grown, and sooner or later, we would have to take her to the vet to have them cut.

"Listen, kids," said Mom, "Kira must have her ears and tail cut. Dogs of this type must have this done. Otherwise, they look ugly when they're grown-up."

Lucia and I did not protest. We knew that we had to take Kira to the vet so he could cut whatever he had to cut. Afterward, he would return to us the most beautiful of all the dogs, with vaccines and all. Neither Lucia nor I could imagine how painful this type of surgery was for puppies.

Our joy, unfortunately, was not lasting. One day, Kira woke up with a stomachache. We didn't know what had made her sick. Lucia, very sad, said that Kira had gotten ill because she had eaten Mother's flowers. I didn't know what to say or think. I only felt uneasy because Kira was ill.

After Mom had been taking care of Kira for two consecutive days, and the pup hadn't stopped having diarrhea and vomiting, Mom and Dad decided to return her to Carmella, the woman who had sold her to us. Dad told Lucia and me not to worry about anything because Carmella's son was a vet, and he would make sure that nothing bad would happen to our pet.

"Kira's mother lives in Carmella's house," Mom said. "Once she's well, I will bring her back to you."

It was very sad for me and Lucia to think that our puppy was going to leave our home, and that we would probably not see her again. Lucia was unable to hold back her tears, and she ran upstairs to her room.

"Poor Kira, Arturo. I don't want anything to happen to her. I just want her to get well," Lucia told me.

"I want her to get well, too, so she can play with us again," I told her.

So, we could do nothing else but pet our poor puppy before Mom and Dad put her into the car to take her away. In that instant, I could only remember Kira in her basket sleeping and showing her reluctance to do anything because of her physical indisposition. "Poor little thing, you must be feeling bad," I told the puppy.

From the time Kira left our house, I had a series of thoughts that made me fervently wish that someone (perhaps a neighbor) was guilty of my puppy's illness. In my opinion, there had to be someone responsible for Kira's situation. The problem at that time consisted of determining who this person was. I told Lucia this series of thoughts that I had in my head, and she told me, to my surprise, that she was not interested in them and that they were senseless. Dad had told her that no one was responsible for Kira's illness, that she had become ill in the same way in which one becomes ill with a cold. It was then that I realized that I could do nothing for my pet except curse a little, fervently wish that she got well, and then constantly ask Mom and Dad about her state of health.

II

Erika's Arrival

Some days after Kira left the house, right before we left for school, my Mom made an announcement.

"Children, today I'll have a surprise for you when you return from school."

"Is Kira well now, Mom?" Lucia asked, full of expectation of once again holding her pup.

"I've told you, it is a surprise, so I won't say anything more. I can only tell you in advance that you will like it very much."

"C'mon, Mom, tell us what it is," Lucia and I begged her. We so wanted to hear that Kira would return home.

Lucia and I realized that Mom would not tell us more, especially because it was getting late for us to leave to school. On the way, my sister and I talked, trying to guess what Mom´s surprise would be. As far as I was concerned, Mother would buy us something, but Kira was not returning home. Otherwise, Mom would have told us ahead of time. Lucia and I were resigned and hopeful that the six or seven hours of classes would go by as quickly as possible. Unfortunately, I couldn't stop thinking of the surprise awaiting us at home after school. On that day, classes were never-ending, and I paid no attention to them whatsoever. To avoid having a problem with my teachers, I tried to look intelligent and interested in what they were saying, while inside, I was going to pieces asking myself multiple questions about what Mom's surprise was. Without knowing it fully, I considered various hypotheses, and made a list in my mind of the possible surprises that Mom could have reserved for us that afternoon. Several times, I thought that one of these hypotheses would be the right response to the question, "What does Mamma have reserved for us as a surprise this afternoon?" It got to be such an obsession that I did what I had sworn I would never do in my life: go and look for Lucia during recess. When I found her, she was coming toward me, and I thought maybe she had the same idea that I had.

Lucia said it was simple: Mom would be waiting for us at home with Kira, completely healthy and well. I told her that I didn't think so, and that Mom's words were quite mysterious. In my view, Mom would have a new pet for us at home, and I knew what it would be. "Mom got us a kitten," I suddenly told myself, not realizing what I was saying. "Lucia, would you like to have a kitten instead of Kira?"

At first, my question lit up my sister's face with joy, but then I saw that she was saddened.

"You know, Arturo, I've become very fond of Kira. All these days, I've wished she'd come back home."

I closed my eyes. There, right in front of me, was my pet, ready to play and obey me. I also imagined that Kira would be waiting impatiently next to the door, waiting to greet us with her barking, leaps, and kisses. The recess bell brought me back to reality. The few hours from recess to when school was out were never-ending and almost impossible to bear. I was hugely relieved when I heard the school bell signaling that classes were over. I picked up my things as quickly as I could to get in line for the school bus that would take me home. Lucia was waiting for me there, and when I saw her, I immediately told her that I knew what Mom's surprise was about.

"Tell me what it is, Arturo," she said to me anxiously.

"It's the kitten that I told you about."

"I don't believe you. Mom is going to have Kira waiting for us at home. You'll see."

"I bet you whatever you want that it is a kitten."

"No, Arturo, Mom knows well that I love Kira a lot. It's going to be her."

"Well, if you don't believe me, I bet you one month's allowance that it is a kitten."

I was sure that Mom would be waiting for us at home with a kitten. On the way home, I got to thinking that it wouldn't be so bad to have a kitten as a pet, if it was one I could play with. When the bus made the turn to reach our house,

Lucia and I were ready to exit. Without even realizing it, she and I fought to see which one of us would leave the bus first. Once we hit the street, we ran full force toward the house, and we found Mom waiting for us at the threshold of the front door. She told us, "Close your eyes, children." Lucia and I tried to cheat, but Mom caught us and said that there would be no surprise then. So we obeyed. When she told us that we could now open our eyes, we saw that she had a boxer puppy in her hands. "Her name is Erika, and she is Kira's little sister," she told us. I knew it. Mom had a new pet for us!

"You owe me one month of your allowance, Lucia," I informed her very happily.

"Not true. You said that Mom was going to have a kitten and not another pup. Don't cheat, Arturo."

I didn't want to argue with her. I was a little disgusted by her words and by the tone of her voice, but just to see my new pet in front of me made me feel that it wasn't worth arguing with her and that maybe I could resort to maternal authority so Lucia would honor her bets. When I saw Mom stretch out her arms, I rushed forward to take Erika, and I hugged her gleefully. My anger disappeared automatically, and it didn't bother me that Kira had not returned home. I had my new friend in my arms. As a clear sign of our friendship, Erika licked my face when I put her near my cheek to feel the softness of her fur. Erika, unlike Kira, had copper-colored fur and a white spot on the right half of her nose.

III

In the Garden

Erika quickly got used to Lucy and me. On the first day, she played with me. I loved to stand in front of her, pinch her ribs, and run off.

In the beginning, she didn't know what this game was about, and I had to bark hard at her, jump two feet from her, stretch my leg to touch her body, and run off. It wasn't until the third try that Erika understood what I wanted her to do, and she came running behind me, wanting to bite my heels. Once she learned this trick, I taught her various others. One of these consisted of putting together little piles of newspapers and making her jump them one by one. On another occasion, I taught her to play football, but the silly thing didn't seem to get it. She would run behind the ball, and once she had it immobilized between her front paws, she wouldn't let it go for anything in the world. No sport can be played like that.

"Erika, you're so dumb. Do you hear me?" I shouted angrily every time she frustrated my attempts at playing football.

I wanted to get her to run with the ball, give it direction, and, at the right moment, pass it to me so I could make a goal. I knew that it could be done because I had seen an ad on TV about a boy and his dog playing like that. It's impossible, I told myself many times, for dog actors to be smarter than my Erika. I had to teach her many tricks. "Sit," I would order her firmly, pointing her to a place on the floor and hoping she would obey. Erika would come near the indicated spot and lie down, lowering her ears. To lie down is not to sit down, but it was humanly impossible to make her understand the difference. I despaired after many tries and, in a fit of rage, told her she'd be punished for two days by not playing with me. I then went to watch TV. Like all other programs, cartoons bored me, which is why I decided, for just this once, to lift Erika's punishment early. I went out with her to play "explorers" in the garden. She went ahead of me and quickly let me know if there was any redskin coming. That part of the game went on without any problem, and she stayed ahead of me all the time. The difficulties started when Erika did not come to me to report her findings. To top it all off, she began to jump all over Mom's flowers. I immediately thought that when Mom saw that mess, she would beat Erika so she would not damage her flowers again.

"Mom, did you see how badly that dog, who doesn't obey, behaved?" I asked her when I saw her watching us from the garden door.

"Arturo, all damage caused by Erika when she is under your care, I will claim directly from you with your father's belt," she told me in a threatening tone of voice.

"I was put out. Why should I get a beating if I hadn't done anything wrong? I decided to go watch TV again. Erika followed me with difficulty and, for the first time, up the house stairway."

"It seems she goes up one step and comes down two," Mom said, laughing.

IV

In the Dollhouse

Each day, Erika grew and learned new games. Sometimes Lucia would get into the little wooden house that she had. Since Erika went in as a guest, Lucia would arrange all her dolls so they would be presentable and would know how to be grateful for all the courtesies that, according to her, Erika bestowed upon them with her presence. It was an indispensable requirement for those visits for Lucia to find Erika the proper garments.

After rummaging around in her drawers, Lucia said that she already knew what clothes she would use to dress Erika. Ten minutes after Lucia made this announcement, Erika was wearing the same hat with a bow that Kira had once used. As if this weren't enough, one of Lucia's doll's sweaters was stretched over Erika's lumpy body. Under other circumstances, Erika would have laughed, but her scared face and the two or three tears she had under each eye gave the impression that she was suffering from no one knew what cause. With that face and those clothes, Erika made her first visit to Lucia's dollhouse. When she arrived, she behaved well, since she went into the little house in Lucia's arms. She, my sister, took care of and introduced everybody.

"Look, she is Lorena, a well-behaved doll. Ah, but there is Georgina. She is an annoying doll. You just put her to sleep, and if she has her batteries on, she tells you, 'Mamma, Mamma, I'm hungry.' The other one is Aurora. She likes to dress in many ways. Today, as you can see, she is disguised as a cowgirl. Tomorrow, she must dress as a Brazilian dancer and, the day after, as a *China poblana* with an old traditional Mexican dress. Look, Erika, I'd like to introduce you to

Teresa. She is our schoolteacher, and she likes well-behaved children," my sister told her.

For her part, Erika limited herself to sniffing her new plastic friends. So that she might feel confident, Lucia put her down and sat her between Georgina and Aurora. Erika continued to sniff her new companions. In a moment of distraction for Lucia, a small disaster took place. From sniffing her new friends so much and from the joy of having been presented in society, she urinated discreetly. At first, the damage she caused was imperceptible, but as the puddle grew, Georgina's and Aurora's dresses and legs got wet. When Lucia realized this mishap, she started to cry and ran out of the little wooden house looking for Mother. How was it possible, my sister asked herself, that Erika could be so rude and not beg pardon from her new friends for her terrible offenses?

V

THE ACCIDENT

A day later, Erika had a real bad accident. Everything happened in a confused and hasty manner. As with most accidents, Erika's could have been avoided with a little precaution. On that day, Mom was getting into her car, and Lucia and I were going to stay home. Erika was with us, and she wanted to play and run around in the garden.

"Bye, children," Mom said before she left.

"Bye, Mom," we answered.

Erika, for her part, barked as if she were also saying goodbye. We all smiled, and Erika started to leap and run around in the garden. Lucia and I ran behind her to see which one of us could catch her. Erika understood the game quite well from the start and did not let either of us catch her. Once Mom had taken her car out, the maid came to help us in our game. Unfortunately, she had left the garage door open. Erika, in her forays, reached the door to the street. She waited until Lucia and I were a few steps away from her to begin her race, although this time she headed for the sidewalk toward the unknown.

"C'mon, Erika, don't get down from the sidewalk," Lucia yelled at her, highly distressed.

Erika thought the game was still on and ran toward the sidewalk facing her. My sister and I began to get nervous. I felt my heart beating fast. At that moment, Lucia saw from afar that a white car was coming near.

"She is going to get run over if she crosses the street," Lucia said, overcome with fear.

At that instant, when my sister expressed her fears, Erika decided to make her way back home. As she ran toward us, we saw that the car first hit her with the fender on one side, and then we saw how she was hit several times with the lower part of the car. Lucia and I saw, with our hearts in our mouths, that, fortunately, a tire had not passed over her. We breathed a sigh of relief when we saw Erika get up and go toward the house, limping to hide in her basket. Lucia observed that she was trembling but did not dare touch her. Erika did not bark or howl, but there she was in her basket, not moving, with her eyes upon us. I tried to touch her to carry her and calm her down. I just slightly touched her front right leg when she began to bark endlessly in a high pitch that scared Lucia and me very much.

"Arturo, do you think that Erika is going to die on us like Kira?" Lucia asked me, trying to hold her tears back.

"Don't be so dumb, Lucia. You always say very dumb things," I told her, just to have something to say. I didn't know how to answer her since her comment made me think of the possibility that I'd be without a pet once again. In my head, I couldn't bear the thought of losing Erika.

"Look, dumb-dumb, better call Aunt Rebecca so she can come and help us with Erika until Mom comes back," I said without realizing that she had already run off to make the phone call.

For half an hour until my aunt arrived, I devoted my time to petting Erika on her head. It was the only place that did not bother her, and she let me do it.

"Look, children, if your mother sees you with those long and sad faces, she'll be angry at me," said Aunt Rebecca. "So, we better take Erika to the vet, and you change the expression on your faces because nothing is going to happen to your pet."

Lucia and I were very sad on our trip to the vet. A thousand terrible things went through my mind about what could happen to Erika. I thought they would operate on her and that she would not survive that operation, and then I thought, among other things, that the vet would only prescribe some medicine for her, so we could all return home running as if nothing had happened.

"Your puppy is going to be like new. Of course, she will not be able to run for the next two weeks," the vet told us when he handed her to us with her leg in a cast.

"I knew it would be nothing serious," Lucia said joyfully.

When I saw Erika with her leg in a cast, with her sad eyes, certain that everything was over, I felt a huge weight coming off my back. My dog would not abandon me, I told myself. My dog and I, I told myself again, would be together in the good and the bad. I wanted to carry her, but I was scared of hurting her. I was resigned to seeing how Lucy would pet her head, and she began to doze off on the way home. There was a moment in which I imagined that Erika was smiling at us and telling us, "Everything's over, you all. Don't worry. Let's go home and wait for Mom to arrive." Before getting out of the car and thanking Aunt Rebecca, I told my sister, "We are going to have to watch her very carefully, Lucia."

"Yes," she answered me, and I watched as she went inside the house, hugging Erika as she had never hugged any of her dolls before.

VI

The Popsicle Store

Close to the house, there was a popsicle store, and my sister and I loved to go with Erika to buy our ice cream and popsicles there. To tell the truth, Erika was the one who most liked to take those walks there. Erika, because of a series of several events had acquired a liking for lemon and strawberry popsicles.

The first time that Erika tasted these delicacies was when Lucia and I were sharing a popsicle. Lucia bit off a very big bite of it and sort of loosened it on one side. The popsicle fragmented, and a piece fell onto the floor. Erika came near the piece of ice, sniffed it, and began to lick it. Lucia and I thought that she was not going to like it, because it was a piece of ice with flavor. We were wrong. In a few seconds, she ate up the popsicle piece that had fallen. Immediately afterward, Erika stood up on two legs and leaned on my trousers to ask me—or rather bark at me—to give her more of this delicious dessert.

"Erika, we have no more money. We can't buy another popsicle," I told her, showing her my empty trouser pockets.

She would not listen to reason and continued to bark.

"I'll sell you a popsicle on credit, but you come and pay me later. It is not the first dog that begs for another popsicle that I make," the store clerk told us. Lucia and I thought that he had added the last part with a touch of pride that he could not hide.

Every Saturday morning, Erika would seek me out and bark insistently and stand up on my trousers. This was her way of asking me to buy popsicles.

Lucia and I also liked these strolls. Erika was already a large and robust dog who instilled fear and respect in many people, and we felt safe and protected when walking down the street with her. Mom and Dad always looked on with approval when she accompanied us. Just like us, they thought that no one would bother us when our dog was present.

One day, when I went to visit a school friend, I suffered a mishap about which I told Dad. It was about an intent to steal my watch. When Erika realized that a stranger was pulling on my arm, she lunged at the aggressor. Dad told me to take Erika every time Lucia and I went for a walk. "She'll protect you at all times," was what Dad said.

From the time of that incident, I noticed that Mom and Dad frequently called Erika and that they took her to the rear of the garden. There, they both played with her, and Dad made her do some exercises and would tell her, patting her on her sides, that every time she went out with us, to watch over us. I do think that Erika understood well what Dad was telling her on these occasions, since, as of that moment, she never allowed any stranger on the street to come near us. All of us at the house felt very proud of our guardian dog.

"Every time you go out on the street, go to the popsicle store and buy Erika a lemon popsicle because she deserves it for taking care of you," Mom would tell us frequently. If Erika just heard the words "popsicle store" or "popsicle," she would start barking with joy. The only thing lacking was for her to tell us what flavor she wanted us to buy her.

VII
The Latest News

Erika grew, and so did we. She was our companion in innumerable games and activities. She was, in a word, a sister to Lucia and me. To tell the truth, many times I preferred Erika, because Lucia, on many occasions, was a dumb and dull sister who got annoyed at everything. On the other hand, Erika was not as complicated as Lucia was. She obeyed me right away and was always willing to keep me company.

While Lucia and I were on our way to becoming adolescents, Erika was beginning to get old. Abrupt climatic changes affected her rheumatism. In rainy weather, we could see how she limped on the leg that she had broken when the car ran into her. Little by little, she had gray hairs around her nose, and there even came a time when we realized that she became sad at anything and everything. Many times, what could have been a playful reprimand would cause tears to roll down from her eyes.

"Erika is getting old," Mom would tell us, not so much to make us understand that she was becoming an elderly dog but, rather, as a small sign of affection and worry because of her advanced years.

When I finished my sophomore year in engineering, I won a scholarship to study English in the United States for two months. At first, all was excitement and joy in our home.

"I've never won anything, and now this boy surprises me with his scholarship," Dad said. "I'm very happy that Arturo is beginning to look out for himself."

Even though everyone at home was happy about my scholarship, I think that Erika didn't like the idea that I would be absent for such a long time. However, I didn't pay any attention to the fact that she was more taciturn than ever from the moment I announced my trip to the United States. On the day my plane was leaving, I went to say goodbye to her.

"Erika, I'll be back in a few weeks. I want you to watch out for Dad, Mom, and Lucia. I also want you to take care of yourself. Don't be running around in the house. You are no longer at an age to do crazy things. Do you promise to be obedient? I'm going to miss you very much," I told her while petting her on the head.

I realized that Erika was very sad. "Let's hope that she'll get over it soon," I told myself to make her state of mind less important. She licked my face as she had always done since we were little and wanted to play with me. From the car, I could tell that she was watching me go with sadness, and I tried to pretend I was happy. "Go on, don't be so dumb. Take advantage of this trip," I remember telling myself moments before I got on the plane.

When the plane was returning home, I had great hopes of seeing the whole family together. I felt a great desire to hug Mom, Dad, and Lucia. Erika would only get a few pats on her back, and then I would pet her on the head. I wanted to see my whole family. It had been two months since I had been unmindful of everything, of my engineering studies and my friends, and I called home once a week. Now, I would have to call my friends and enjoy the few vacation days remaining. In a few words, I had to enjoy my return.

I was bringing gifts to the whole family. I had no trouble bringing Dad and Erika their gifts. I was bringing Dad a shaver and Erika a Frisbee so that Lucia and I could play with her. It took hard work and imagination to look for gifts for Mom and Lucia because I didn't know what to get them. I breathed a sigh of relief when I realized that my troubles would be over if I bought each of them perfume.

Once I went through customs, I ran out through the airport entrance to look for Mom and Dad. "Here I am. I've arrived," I shouted at them, not knowing how to contain my joy. It was a happy moment to be able to hug my parents and Lucia. For their part, they were also waiting for me, full of joy and enthusiasm.

On the way home, Mom and Dad wanted me to tell them everything that I had done. I couldn't stop talking.

"How's Erika? I asked them the moment I remembered my dog. "I'm anxious to see her. I missed all of you a lot. I brought a gift for Erika."

While I was talking, I noticed that Lucia was looking intently at the floor of the car, and that her expression became sad.

"What's wrong, Dad?" I asked, a little scared. "Is Erika sick?"

"No, Arturo. What happened was that Erika got sick two weeks ago," Dad said.

"How is she? Did the vet see her?" I asked, excited.

"She died, Arturo," said Mom. "The vet said she died from sadness. Every day she would go into your room and would start looking for you. When she didn't find you, she would lie down beside your bed and start to cry. We all did what we could to distract her, but she paid no attention to us and cried about everything." My Mom told me all of this unhurriedly, as if she were choosing every word carefully. She seemed to have in mind everything Erika had done in my absence.

I was very saddened by what Mom had told me. I knew that Erika was an old dog who could die at any time. But I had never prepared myself mentally for this moment.

"I feel as if one of us had died, Mom," I said, trying to contain my emotions.

"Me, too, Arturo," Lucia said.

My sister took me by the hand and hid her face. I thought that Lucia and I would talk extensively about our feelings and memories when we got home. For the moment, Erika's presence made us keep silent.

VIII
The Invitation

Dear and Beloved Erika,

Arturo and I want to wish you all the best on this, your birthday. Mom says that a year ago today, you arrived at our home, which is why today is also your anniversary. Arturo and I have argued about the best way to celebrate your day. The dumb-dumb wanted us to get you a birthday cake! I told him how dumb he was because dogs like to eat bones. Arturo continued to behave badly and was stubborn, so I decided to celebrate this with you alone. I thought you might like to spend the day in our little wooden house. Georgina and Aurora have told me that they forgave you for your prank the other day. "We can hardly remember that time when Erika got our dresses wet," they both told me. I asked Mom to buy you two pounds of bones with my allowance money and to prepare them just like she knows you like them. Be sure to come to the little house. We expect you at 4:30 (which is after lunch). I send you a kiss.

Sincerely,
Lucy

P.S. Georgina and Aurora asked me to tell you that they want you to behave properly. They, as does the whole family, love you a lot.

UXMAL AND CELESTUN

I

UXMAL

(A Spider, a Japanese Man, and Archaeological Ruins)

I had promised my daughter that I would take her on a trip. "A marvelous one of eco-tourism," I remember telling her. When I talked about this family plan in the office, Carlos, a companion from Merida, Yucatan, suggested that I visit Celestun. I had heard very little about Celestun, and I must say that the name attracted me. I looked up a bit about the place and said to myself, "Why not go first to Merida and then from there to Celestun and some Mayan ruins?"

"Javier, you don't need to go to Costa Rica. Better go to Yucatan, to Celestun," I remember Carlos telling me in a firm voice. And that's what I did. I planned the trip in detail, and once we were situated in the hotel in Merida, we went to pick up the car that I had reserved to make the run that we had planned.

On our first day there, we went to visit Uxmal. I remember that the main pyramids of that Mayan city reflected a stylized architecture of forms and fine shapes, rich in detail. I also remember that the decoration of the walls of the buildings was balanced and in equilibrium. There was no border or carved stone on one side if it wasn't also on the other side. Border, stone, and shape came together on the walls of the buildings to enrich the sight, to give the idea that before the construction was started, someone had already thought about the place for each thing, from a carved stone to a monumental palace. Not only is there harmony in the structures, but they also give you the impression that they were thought out to be easily and quickly integrated into the vegetation, into the green landscape. If one walks down the back of the ruins, one can see the many huge and luxuriant trees with dazzling crowns. From the top of the ruins, the trees look as if they have always been inhabitants of the place, taking care of what remains of the impressive Mayan cities. On the one side, the green of the vegetation predominates, and on the other, the gray of the stones. One must go to Uxmal and see how the natives of the place, with tools that possibly were quite rudimentary, were able to give shape and life to the stones and build a majestic pre-Hispanic city.

Amid the admirable spectacle that is Uxmal, two characters stand out. One of them is a spider the size of an extended hand. Its body and legs are completely black, and at several feet in the distance, it seems that this arachnid is an entirely hairy being. A few feet in front of the animal, there is a Japanese man who is filming it, engrossed with a large video camera. The two beings are on the entryway to the ruins toward the main buildings, and the large spider is on the stone wall of a little ramp. The photographer and the large spider have hypnotized one another. Neither of the two changed position during the more than two hours that passed from the time we went into the place until when we left it. This great Mayan spider will be immortalized in many videos that will circulate in Tokyo. It could be that it would accompany some figure of Buddha as a sample of a possible, or maybe of an inevitable, future reincarnation of some afflicted human being.

This spider, with or without the help of an enlightened person or a photographer, is already immortal because it is the being that cares day and night for the temples and ruins of Uxmal. When the sun goes down, it comes out to make its run. From the place where it lives in the entrails of the exuberant vegetation, it goes toward the buildings and the rooms that the noble Mayans occupied in days gone by. Upon daybreak, self-assured and with honor, it goes up the stairs of the palaces where before, only the chosen ones could come near. Today, just like yesterday, and as always, it will climb up speedily, coordinating the movement of all its legs, up to the highest part of the ruins. From the heights, it will tell the world that there, in Uxmal or wherever the immortal video is exhibited, there are two fabulous marvels. One was made by the hand of man that gave shape to this majestic Mayan city; the other was the creation of some unknown god of the region, who, before disappearing forever—dragged by the fury of the wind—was eager to give shape, movement, and life to a fabulous stone that someone had left at the entrance of the place so it could become an immortal sentry with a balanced shape of many black legs.

II

CELESTUN

(Birds and Iguanas)

Celestun is located to the east of Merida. It is said that in Mayan, Celestun means the place of stones. The internet says that part of this place, lying on the Gulf of Mexico side, is a fishing port, where the traveler can enjoy feasting on its delicious shrimp and other shellfish, which is true. A peculiarity of this part of Celestun is that the setting sun can be seen on the sea from there. It is said that it is one of the few places on the solid ground of Yucatan that this is so because, in all the other places, the sun hides behind the luxuriant trees. Aside from this fact, the setting of the sun was superb. The photograph, which we took, shows an orange-reddish tone in a large part of the heavenly canopy right before sunset. Perhaps this sunset is comparable in color, beauty, and majesty to that which takes place an hour later on the Pacific Ocean side in Cabo San Lucas.

This comparison arises from the memory that I have of the time we went out to the marina of Cabo San Lucas onboard a large vessel with the intent of sighting whales. The vessel first came near the rocks and the arch on which the Baja California peninsula disappears to give way to the sea. On the way, we saw the colony of sea lions living on the steep, rugged rock facing the arch, and then the vessel headed to make the turn toward the open Pacific Ocean. Unfortunately, I did not see any cetacean, even though my daughter maintains that, on two occasions, she did see the back of an enormous whale. From afar, one could see that the sea got lost in the horizon line. A little before late afternoon, the lower part of the sky began to change color and take on reddish-orange shades in bands. As the sun began to set, these bands became more intense. The vessel, on its way back to the marina, went right past the arch. What a marvelous sight! Through the arch or the stone window it is, we had an unforgettable view of the other side of the sea. The change in shades of the sky could also be seen on the other side of the arch at the moment of the sunset.

The battery ran out on our camera, so we could no longer use it. My daughter was then using her cell phone camera. There, one can see a thin, orange-colored band dressing up the nudity of the arch: Celestun and Cabo San Lucas, first one and then the other, painted orange and reddish shades on the horizon. One can think that Celestun lent its colors to Cabo San Lucas; that is, its lipstick and its makeup powder so that both places could wear it with dash and charm in a public act. Its pink shades are colored exactly alike at the moment of the sunset or the moment the sun embraces the horizon with passion, fire, and tenderness.

The other part of Celestun is the estuary, where the flamingoes live, as do the black ducks that come from afar to spend the winter at that place, the many white and gray herons, and some small marine birds, appealing, with long feet, that the villagers call beach penguins. On the estuary, far from the coming and going of the boats and close to the shore, one can see colonies of flamingoes forming wide circles. The flamingoes not only socialize this way, and they also take advantage of coming together to eat shrimp larvae. According to what our guide told us, when young, these birds have dark feathers, and as they grow and feed on shrimp, the color of their feathers changes little by little until they turn pink. We asked the pilot to take the boat near where the flamingoes were. He told us he could not do that because the place where the birds were was not deep enough, and that was why we could see some of them erect and standing on their feet and others with their legs bent. The guide tried to bring the boat as close as he could. Then he turned off the motor. We were still at a distance from the flamingoes, although now, amid our silence, we heard from afar their daily conversations between croak and croak.

Once we had observed several flamingo groups, the boat took us to where the estuary and Gulf meet. At the very end of that minute peninsula, we saw the beach penguins. They looked like bathers chatting where the smallest waves broke. To one side of these birds, other larger ones stood as if they were watching them, like older brothers. Then, the boat took us to the other coastline of the estuary so we could visit the petrified forest. This is found in part of the continental mass of the Yucatan peninsula that, for some strange reason, began to fill up with saltwater. At first, many trees dried up, and then they were petrified. Now they are grey trunks—which get very thin at their tops—with almost no branches. At any moment, what is left of their roots will no longer hold them up, and they will fall heavily to the ground, as some trees have, which are now lying inert and a little rotted away on the ground.

We saw two iguanas on the upper part of one of those gray, lifeless sticks. I do not know if this is a natural matter or if the iguana, the same as its close relative the chameleon, changes color. The two iguanas must have been adult animals and must have measured around seventy or eighty centimeters long. They were motionless, as they possibly had been for thousands of years as evolution passed them by, never noticing them to even consider the possibility of making them a little prettier, less quiet, and perhaps more sociable.

We paid attention, and we noticed that high on a dying tree (this one was only partly petrified because it still had some green branches), there was a solitary iguana. It was motionless and intent on looking toward the estuary. It gave the impression of being the iguana that was watching to see that everything was in order in and out of the water. It didn't take notice of us. It seemed that its mission was to preserve the site and once again make Celestun the place of millenary harmony, of the water that flows forever, as well as to preserve the safe refuge of birds and reptiles it has always been. Everything indicated that the main task of the iguana was to be watchful, so that with the passing of the years, the stones were never worn down or dragged away by the interminable flow of water because they must always be the sacred stones of the estuary. Otherwise, and without the iguana's vigilance, the birds would die, and Celestun would disappear in painful agony, such as the one lived by the trees that today are petrified.

BIRDS, FOXES, AND HERONS OF SAN MIGUEL DE ALLENDE

I

WOODPECKERS

It is early in the morning, a Sunday, and I am having breakfast on the terrace of the Corazon Inn. From this place, one can almost see the whole garden of this bed and breakfast. That means that I have a view before me of several very large and luxuriant trees and of one that stands out for having few branches with leaves. Perhaps the tree is drying up, although that is not what is important. What is relevant is that it is a training workshop for two woodpeckers. One of them is now on the high part of the trunk, almost at the top of the tree. It uses its beak to drill the wood of the tree. It does so furiously, as if it and the trunk had a pending dispute—an affront to be resolved. One part pierces with ire and force, and the other resists with strength and dignity.

The other bird is on a large branch, and its back is to the ground. Due to this, I imagine, it grasps the tree with all the strength of its legs so as not to fall off. If it were to let go and fall from the branch, there would be no accident because, fortunately, this small animal with wings knows it can fly with great dexterity. For this reason, there would never be a mishap when its legs do not hold it to a branch.

A few days ago, I also saw a bird upside down, held by a branch. This was in the interior garden of the house, and that winged being was a very small one, and I am sure a very playful one. That small bird had reached the interior garden of the house, accompanied by some eight or ten more of those little birds. Together with its companions, it inspected the ivy and the three trees that we had planted there. It got hold of a branch of the ivy, and in a wink, it got upside down alone. Who knows what it was looking at from that uncomfortable position? I noticed that its whole body was hanging from its legs. It was there looking for some seconds, and then it decided to go flying. As it did so, it flung itself into the air, spinning its body to retake the normal flying position, and then quickly extended its wings. This small bird turned out to be a true Olympic gymnastics champion. First, it showed great strength, as the best gymnasts do who work on the rings. Second, it demonstrated an advanced and complex technique—to come out well from having flung itself into the air—that all gymnasts who do routines and exercises on the asymmetric bars would envy, particularly its exit routine.

Going back to the woodpeckers, one can see that each of them is concentrating on its own matters, and neither has gone to inspect the work of the other. I am sure that I am in the presence of two carpentry and architecture professionals who already have fixed in their minds and their wings the house design they want to build. No human power could draw them away from their concentration while they are diligently providing shape and form to their architectural ideas on the part of the trunk that will be their home, sweet home.

While observing the spectacle of the two woodpeckers, I realized that two other birds of another species were fluttering nearby. These two birds were larger than the two woodpeckers; their chests were of a light-yellow color, and nature had endowed them with potent vocal cords so they could sing. The waiter at the Corazon Inn, after asking if I liked to watch birds, told me that a few days earlier, he had seen a whole tree full of woodpeckers. "You can't imagine what a beautiful sight that was," he told me. I believed him, and I imagined that a group of persevering, winged engineers and future spouses had arrived from the University of Life to undertake intensive construction practices of one-family wooden homes.

Possibly, two of the birds that the waiter had seen a few days earlier were now in the garden of this agreeable inn. The tenacity, dedication, and effort shown by those two birds there on the tree in front of me were no more than a reflection of the new responsibilities that they had acquired as new husbands. These male birds also knew that they would soon be happy, important, and responsible fathers, with at least a pair of beautiful and hungry little chicks. These broods would need a pretty home to live in, like the ones those two hard-working and future father birds are building with enthusiasm and the best of themselves: their imaginative and powerful beaks.

II

A Fox, a Vixen, and a Roadrunner

Some years ago, we went to El Charco del Ingenio for the first time. It is a botanical garden situated in the northeast of downtown San Miguel de Allende. It was the first time we had gone to that place, and we made it a point to walk through its numerous footpaths. One of these took us to the plant conservatory, a metallic and translucent vault where we found various small and large cactus plants. My attention was drawn to the large variety of this type of vegetation. There was one cactus that was about six feet high, the central part of which was an elongated curved stem. Across this plant, adjoining its mass, was an enormous and extended white beard, like cotton. Inside the conservatory were many more cacti, large (maxi) and small (mini).

We left the plant conservatory and continued our excursion. We walked through more footpaths and went toward Las Colonias Dam, which divides the botanical garden from the ecological reserve that makes up El Charco del Ingenio, and Landeta Park, a green area adjacent to El Charco. At the dam, we saw some white ducks that, judging from their size and weight, one could guess were well fed. We continued our walk, and more than noticing the flowers and the trees, of which there were many, we were thinking about where some of the water in the dam drained. When coming around a curve in the footpath, we found a gray fox facing us at about 30 yards.

I think the fox was crossing from one side of El Charco to another when it heard a noise, and then it paused to see what living being or species was making it. It watched us three—my daughter, my wife, and me—cautiously and then quickly disappeared into the bushes. We again took up our walk, and a few minutes later, on another footpath, we found a roadrunner. Its feathers were a dark gray, and when it saw that we were a group of three people going up a slope, it decided, like a theater character, to abandon the scene. It made a half turn and moved ahead, taking four large leaps or strides while it extended its wings. Immediately afterward, we saw it flying away toward the dam and getting lost among the trees.

We were not surprised to see animals roaming around freely at El Charco because, as we were going into the ecological reserve, the man in charge had told us that we could find some animals on the way. I thought he was referring to turtles, since before he made this comment, we had seen how a young American couple was donating a melon-sized turtle to that place. They said that they had found it in the garden of the house where they were staying and thought that this reptile would live much better at El Charco del Ingenio. They left the turtle and took away the bucket in which they had brought it.

Two years later, we again visited El Charco del Ingenio. On this occasion, my daughter and I were walking through one of the many footpaths of the place, from a section where there are rocks high up and from where one has a complete view of the town of San Miguel and of the cultivated fields that are on the way to Dolores, Hidalgo. The fields were green, making the view most agreeable. We were already heading toward the exit when a vixen came out with her tail coiled on the footpath where we were walking. The little vixen was a little more than five yards ahead of us and happily accompanied us on our course. She was wagging her tail a little and in no hurry as she led us through the dirt roads of the place for some 50 yards.

Maybe the little vixen remembered that she had something pending; at the least expected moment, she abandoned the little road and our company—without even saying, "With your leave, I'll be back with you in a minute," or "It was a pleasure to meet you, I was enchanted"—and got lost in the bushes. Our rude and impolite companion not only abandoned us hurriedly, but she also failed to say goodbye. Her rudeness and lack of consideration were obvious as well because she had always turned her back on us.

III

SWALLOW CHICK

Back then, my daughter was almost twelve years old, and at the Angels' Mission Hotel in San Miguel de Allende, in addition to people, they also allowed swallow families to lodge there. It was common to find the nests of these birds in the high parts of the walls of the corridors or on the cornices of the hotel, where vaults and arches emerge. In 1997, they assigned us to a villa, and next to the upper part of its door, there was a nest. When we arrived, we could hear the swallows chirping and saw how Mama and Papa swallow flew away to search for food for their family.

When we returned to the hotel one afternoon after taking a walk to San Miguel, we found that a chick from our nest (or from the one at the entrance of our villa) had fallen onto a lamp. That lamp was a light bulb that stuck out upward from a high cornice. The lampshade of that lamp was a kind of glass flower vase that was round, thin, elongated, and open on both ends. The chick was close to the light bulb, and God only knew how it fell on that light and heat trap. The three of us, my daughter, my wife, and I, realized that the chick could die from the excessive heat of the lightbulb or malnutrition.

The chick's parents fluttered from one side to the other at the entrance of our villa, not understanding what had happened to their chick or knowing what to do to rescue it from the mishap it was in. We brought out a bench from the villa on which I stood since the cornice (where the lamp that had caught the chick was located) was in a high place. First, I struggled not to fall off the bench then to detach the bottom of the glass lampshade. There were some plier-type metal handles that I had to loosen to completely detach the lampshade so I could rescue the chick. But every time I detached a handle, the grimy bench on which I was standing shook strongly. I told myself that if I got careless, I would have a tremendous fall. Finally, I was able to remove the glass lampshade, pick up the chick, give it to my wife and, lastly, place it carefully in its nest—all of this, obviously, under the scrutiny of its parents.

I did not fall at any time, but I felt that all my movements were being watched by the heedful look of my daughter. We had to save the chick (that I knew): I had to be the means that would allow this to happen (I also knew that). And this whole story of concern by the parents of the chick, my daughter, my wife, and me had to have a happy ending (that I did not know). Fortunately, the ending was happy. When I placed the chick in its mud and hay cradle, I told it—not with words, but with my thoughts—as if we were great friends and was asking him for a favor, "Little bird, don't be leaving your nest. Pity me. Can't you see that if I fall from this shaky bench, I will break my neck, and there will be nobody that can once again rescue you from this horrible, hot, and boiling light bulb that is only good for roasting little birds that had an accident?"

The chick understood me. It behaved well, and during the days that we continued to stay at the hotel, it did not have any further mishaps or setbacks of any kind. Every time we left or arrived at the villa, I had the sensation or intuition that someone was greeting us with a very low and thin voice, saying good day or good afternoon. Every time I looked to see who had done it, I found a chambermaid that greeted me from afar or another hotel guest who was coming down the corridor, bowing his head, and possibly murmuring something. What turned out to be somewhat disquieting about these greetings was the tone of voice of the one who had made them: it was very thin, much like the soft chirping of a sad and shy little bird.

IV

HUNGRY HERONS

Juarez Park of San Miguel de Allende celebrated its first centennial in 2004. This means that it has large trees, beautiful plants, and an intrusive colony of white herons, which have resisted leaving the place. According to some San Miguel townspeople, one fine day, numerous white herons arrived at the Ignacio Allende Dam. It is believed that they had come from somewhere on the coastline, and they had gotten lost on their way. From the air, the birds saw the dam, the enormous trees of Juarez Park, and the town church. The pretty view made them say, "Home Sweet Home," and without any apparent setback, they installed themselves in the treetops of Juarez Park.

Although herons are intrusive animals, paratroopers, and unwelcome characters for the trees in that park (their dung is quite acid and damages the roots of all the trees), they have adapted with great ease to life in San Miguel. For example, at one time, the San Miguel townspeople wanted them to abandon the site, and to this end, they organized an attack with firecrackers to frighten them. They say that the result was a pretty and traditional spectacle, with lots of thunderclaps from the firecrackers but not too effective in its original purpose. The herons temporarily moved to another address; then, they went back home with no inconvenience after the firecracker party ended. Later, somebody in the town had the idea of taking some electric saws and cutting down the high part of the treetops so that the herons would no longer inhabit that place anymore. That operation turned out to be a failure, since the treetops now look somewhat empty, although with the pretty—or horrible, depending on whether you favor them or not—white herons still in their heights.

I believe that the war against the herons is lost. If the San Miguel townspeople could think up something today, they would win a battle. The herons, knowing that strategy counts for everything in life, would step back for a moment and then regroup tomorrow. A few days later, they would be back in their home sweet home, which is the park.

Why do I think that the herons would win the war and not the astute San Miguel townspeople? For one, simple, practical, and easy-to-understand reason. Some years ago, I was walking in El Chorro, a very pretty, typical place, one block from Juarez Park that also has huge luxuriant trees. My wife, daughter, and I were walking when suddenly half of a rather small fish fell in front of our feet. Up above was a heron that looked a little awkward. I think it swallowed only half of the meal it had fished for that day in the Ignacio Allende Dam. This flying animal did not realize that when it bit the head so hard of the fish it had in its beak, some of it had fallen to the ground, for reasons explained by Mr. Newton. As I said, I looked up at the trees. There, as I mentioned, I discovered a sad heron that was looking at us, not understanding what had happened. In addition, I was sure that it had not passed the elementary physics course. I don't know what it decided to do—if it flew toward the dam once again, some kilometers away, and tried to trap another unwary fish, or if, on the other hand, it decided to wait for us to leave the place before it came down to pick up forty percent of its food for that day.

If I were a heron, I would never leave that place. Juarez Park is an incredible nook of peacefulness and beauty. Also, since it is close to the dam, fishermen, like herons, can obtain fabulous, fresh-water dishes. Any heron can enjoy these delicious fish, although one bird clumsily and naively shared its meal with a group of three intruders who were happily walking past the trees. In the end, these were three ungrateful pests that don't know what a friendly invitation to eat fish is in San Miguel.

A Pelican in Puerto Vallarta

I don't remember well whether my wife and I went to Puerto Vallarta on that occasion or whether my daughter went with her maternal grandparents when she was three years old. I was not present at the incident with the poor pelican in either case. According to what I was told, the main characters were my father-in-law and an anonymous pelican with a kind face. I would say that it was a pelican with a good guy's face. But if my daughter reads this, she will start criticizing me for my inaccuracy. She will say that those birds are not people but pelicans, and that some have a good guy's face and some have a bad guy's face. That is simple. In short, this focus could be a simple way of dividing the world by the appearance of the faces of the beings that live in it, regardless of whether they are people or pelicans.

My father-in-law was a great sportsman. As a young man, he played on a water polo team, and he claimed to have swum across a vast lake on several occasions. So it was that a grandpa sportsman was on the beaches of Puerto Vallarta with his wife and his granddaughter. He was doing and thinking of doing everything my daughter asked him to do.

At that time, my daughter was small, and she got emotional the moment she saw a pelican floating in the sea. I don't know what she said or how she said it, but my father-in-law never gave it much thought. He jumped into the sea and swam quickly in the direction of the poor pelican. Several feet before reaching the gentle guy with the face of a good pelican, my father-in-law went underwater. He swam and submerged to where the bird was. He surprised it by taking it by its lower extremities with one hand and pulling it underwater. With his other hand, he held it by the beak. Just like that, he took the surprised seabird close to his granddaughter so that she could see, from a short distance, what a pretty pelican gently floating in the sea looked like. Once he got his wish, and my daughter saw this marine bird close up, my father-in-law let the bird go free. People from Vallarta say that the frightened pelican flew and flew, not resting night or day, until he got to the southern islands of the Pacific Ocean. It sought to take refuge in a faraway place, somewhere without thoughtless and athletic grandfathers who wanted to please their little granddaughters by going around on the beaches of Puerto Vallarta, scaring innocent and well-behaved pelicans.

A Hummingbird

It was December and a few days before Christmas. Some days before that, we had gone to buy the Christmas tree, and we had found a very fragrant pine full of branches. As in past years, my wife and daughter decorated the tree with red Christmas balls. One could swear that it was a tree full of red flowers from afar. It was so showy that I bet my bottom dollar that the little pine tree, so disguised, stimulated the poor hummingbird's curiosity, who ended up trapped in the mouth of Bausi, our schnauzer, because of an unforgivable distraction.

I imagine that the hummingbird saw the red balls on the tree from afar, drawing its attention. It must also have perceived the smell of fresh pine and thought (well, I don't know if it thought anything, but it behaved as *if* it did) that there would be some kind of flower from which it could suck some nectar. The little tree was near a door that led to an interior garden that we always kept open during the day. That is how the hummingbird flew into the house without realizing it when it was inspecting the pine tree. I think it must have been examining the balls, which it thought were dry flowers, one by one, when, in a moment of total distraction, Bausi arrived from behind. Our dog moved without making any noise and, with its remarkable agility, snapped its jaws at the hummingbird and trapped it in its mouth.

I estimate that I happened upon the scene no more than 30 seconds after the little bird became trapped in that unusual and ferocious canine prison. I had just come home, and I had to walk toward the stairs to get to the upper floor. At that moment, I saw that the little dog was walking quite slowly in the living room, not making any noise. I thought that was strange because I knew that it had seen me, and normally when that happened, it would rush to meet me, breaking into barks that were more like howls of pleasure. Its lack of effusiveness on this occasion was strange, so I went near it.

I soon realized that a pointy object was sticking out of its mouth, but I couldn't tell what it was. "Oh, God," I told myself, "this dog swallowed something, getting it stuck in its throat. I must get it out before it damages the dog's insides." I called out to the dog in a sharp voice. "Bausi, spit out that bone!" The dog looked at me, and I saw that its eyes indicated anything but pain. Then, in a sharper way, I ordered it again to spit out what it had in its mouth. Bausi obeyed me. I was surprised at the outcome: it did not spit out a bone or a sharp object, but a hummingbird. I picked up the little bird from the ground, seeing that it was alive. Its tiny heart was swelling wildly in its chest, and I felt it beat between my fingers. The hummingbird extended only one of its wings, and I saw how its green feathers changed their color according to the angle of the light they received. This was worthy of drawing one's attention. I caressed the hummingbird's head and back, and I felt that it did not become more uneasy than it was already. On the tip of the index finger of my left hand, which I had on its little chest, I felt the strong beats of its heart. Due to the great fright that the little bird had undergone, its heart was beating many times per second with huge force.

I went upstairs to show my wife and daughter the hummingbird I had rescued. They were on the roof because they had gone to check on a TV antenna cable. A few steps from where they were, I told them, "Look what I saved from Bausi's mouth." Then I opened my hand. They saw a hummingbird in my palm that took two seconds to extend its wings. Its heart continued to beat with force, and when it felt free for just an instant, it decided to take advantage of the valuable opportunity to escape and began a swift flight to the south. In its fast and hurried exit, it headed toward a metal fence. We all thought that it would collide with it. It didn't. It rose precisely what was needed to avoid the obstacle at a much-reduced distance. We were astonished to see the tiny flying object moving away from us forever, swiftly to the south.

The hummingbird went away, frightened, and with the fear of death from being in the mouth of an enormous beast. I know that it swore it would never again check to see if Christmas trees had red flowers or balls of that color. It took refuge in a faraway field where there were no flowers. The hummingbird has been in that place without leaving for many years and says it does not know if curiosity killed the cat. Still, it was at the point of dying, thanks to its keen desire to check out the false flowers. It doesn't realize it could have died from this bite from an enormous and terrible beast or from a heart attack from having lived a traumatic experience. But no matter how many times it tells the story, and swears that it happened, no one will believe it.

STALLION

The horse is of great size. It is coming at a gallop. Its back legs push it with force, and it moves its front extremities to give the gallop rhythm and grace. The equine mane is abundant and noticeably long. So, whoever rides it bareback has a lot to hold on to avoid falling off. The horse's tail flies high, pointing to heaven, partly because the horse has moved it so and in part because the wind plays with it like that.

The stallion is keeping its head down to its left. Perhaps it heard its owner calling, but it is difficult for a horse with that energy and presence to have an owner, unless he is very special. This type of stallion is too much of a horse for a normal person to control. Maybe that is why it is galloping alone, in total liberty, with no saddle or bridle. A few minutes ago, people saw it prancing with joy. In the distance, on the dirt road, the reddish-brown filly that it likes was seen for a moment. A horseman who thrust his whip and spurs on it was riding it and taking it full speed to train it in the skillful maneuvers of Mexican horsemen. It is said that it is a good and fine filly. As others also assure, it is obedient and sure of itself when galloping.

The stallion snorted. It could have taken off in a wild and senseless race in search of the filly that would be a magnificent and stimulating company for it, but the horseman riding the filly turned out to be a hindrance. It is better to wait until the filly is brought to a slow trot and has its saddle removed. When the filly has recovered from the race, then both horses can play while racing. For now, the stallion prefers to take a quick spin. By this, it wants to do two things: to make sure that its filly is no longer in view and to look after the lady who knows how to ride it. She will take it by the mane and lead it with great adroitness to places where he can't even imagine. On several occasions, it has been said that L. W., the artist, is her owner.

Today, the owner has the stallion in everyone's view, restless and always full of energy. Tomorrow, the stallion will be on her mind and in the movements of her hand. It will be an equine that is coming at a full-speed gallop. When the stallion sees the fine filly at a distance, it will lower its head, snort, and, with gestures and prancing, ask to be let free, to be let out of the imaginary stable, and to be given life and energy to catch up with the magnificent creature that is waiting at the end of the dirt road.

SIRENS

The last time I visited the Queen Sophia Museum, I went to a gallery on one of the streets that provide access to it. It was there that I bought a small engraving in which the artist decided to draw a rhomboid figure. I do not know why, but the work attracted my attention. The engraving includes the following elements: the sun, the wind, three seagulls barely sketched at a distance, the sea with impressive breaking waves, a siren on the waves, and finally, a comet or kite flying about.

In light blue shades, the siren is holding the rope with which she handles the kite. This half-woman, half-beautiful fish, is playing with the kite; she is doing it with the same dexterity as children have in a windy park that is close to the mountains. When the air blows with force in that place, the girls and boys hoist their enormous rhomboid-shaped kites to great heights. Perhaps the shape of the kite has influenced the artist, making her decide to present her work of art in a rhomboid shape.

It seems that the siren lets go of the kite rope on the engraving. Due to the pressure that the wind imposes on her at the moment, it rises more than expected. I imagine that the kite is made of thin, light plastic since one made of paper would get wet with the seawater and then never rise. It would be useless.

Upon scrutinizing the siren's hair on the engraving, a surprise appears, since her hair is blowing toward the left. The kite in the painting is going toward the right, boosted by the wind, which, at the same time, blows the siren's hair in the opposite direction. This cannot happen. The artist may want to tell us that the wind can blow in opposite directions at the same time just as easily as sirens can exist. That is, the artist suggests that sirens do not exist. I think she's wrong. I know that sirens do exist. I saw them at the end of May 1980 on the beaches of Sitges. It was a group of eight young Swedish or Danish women who were playing volleyball in swimsuits on the beach. They were all taller than I was, and judging from the way they were playing, passing the ball from one to another, they made you understand that they were extraordinarily agile and speedy. Anyone would affirm that they were exceptionally attractive and beautiful women from their physical attributes. That is, they were as beautiful as the most beautiful and affectionate sirens that ever existed.

After they got tired of playing and passing the ball from one side of the net to the other, they all ran together at the same time toward the sea. I noticed that each one of them jumped into the water full of joy, as if she needed to humidify her body in the seawater. From where I was, I could have sworn that their bodies had changed color somewhat and even shape when they got into the saltwater. I saw them swimming fast, and it seemed that they wanted to quickly cross the whole Mediterranean southward. I fell in love with all of them. I do not doubt that they decided to return to Stockholm or Copenhagen swimming from Sitges.

Days later, someone told me he had learned from TV that a group of women of Nordic appearance had been seen swimming rapidly in the Bay of Biscay, close to the coast of France. I thought it might have been my sirens. A week later, I learned that someone else had commented that, according to some satellite pictures in the North Sea, an ancient Swedish or Danish ship had been seen rescuing a group of eight women. That vessel was not fully identified; it was headed toward Iceland but disappeared after entering a fog bank. There was also talk that the ancient boat had not performed a rescue, but rather assisted in a previously scheduled reunion. This affirmation comes from the information indicating that the vessel had stopped for no more than six hours at one set point at certain sea coordinates until the assumed rescue. During the time the ship was inactive, it never hurled its nets into the sea, nor did it intend to realize any fishing operation.

If the above is true, then there is no doubt that this was about sirens that live in the direction of Scandinavian countries. The famous siren of Copenhagen lends proof to this belief, and its sculpture is possibly a nostalgic reminder of the passionate and loving encounter that she had with a regional fisherman. This would lend credence to the idea that the descendants of this character, are in the habit of meeting and departing at certain dates of the year in an ancient boat to realize an indispensable and loving meeting on the high sea.

In Mexico, there is also evidence of the presence of fantastic quasi-women. Proof of this is the Mazatlan´s Siren. The wind blows her hair, in the same manner, as it does with the hair of the siren in the engraving, and the sea takes her to faraway places from which she does not want to return. It is well known that there exists a beautiful siren in the life of every fisherman, and it is also true that these half-women, half-fish, jump into the sea in search of daring men of the sea or land. The fishermen know how to trap the sirens in their powerful and invisible nets. These rare fishing tackles affect the sirens' willpower and transform their bodies until they lose their scales and dorsal fin, causing them endless sighs and a tear or two that mixes with the seawater that always trickles down their faces.

64

BABY TURTLES

The day we arrived at the hotel in San Jose del Cabo, in southern Baja California, our hotel personnel told us to be on the beach a little before sundown because there was a surprise for us. We didn't know what the people at the hotel were talking about, but we decided to go anyway to the meeting place they had indicated to us. There, to our surprise, was a biologist who explained to us that he was going to release a batch of baby turtles onto the beach that afternoon. "I need help from all of you guys", he said. "You will soon know what it feels like to have recently hatched turtles in the palms of your hand. Please follow my instructions and treat the little things with complete care."

The numerous hotel guests who participated in this event gathered behind a line that was drawn on the sand some five meters from where the waves were breaking. Then, each one of us was given a pair of newly hatched baby turtles. They were the size of my ring finger. If one put those little reptiles in the palm of one's hand, one could feel how they moved their four little feet and their heads and how they made a huge effort to walk. Then, when we were given the sign, we all placed the little turtles on the sand, and we saw how these tiny reptiles began to walk, little by little, with great effort, down the sand toward the sea.

My daughter placed Darwin and Planck—that's how she had baptized her two turtles—on the sand, and with anxious looks and cheering, motivated them to walk to where the waves were breaking. It seemed that the noise of the waves drew their attention and attracted them.

The small reptiles that were successful in their crossing were those that, with the initial noise of the waves breaking, had sufficient strength to get there. Even though the waves didn't break, at least they hurled water and got them wet. The seawater not only awakened in the baby turtles an instinct of survival, but it doubled their energy and convinced them to keep on walking with all their strength. The spectacle was marvelous. There were hundreds of turtles walking on the sand with great difficulty and filing slowly toward the water in what was a short and slow walk to the next stage in their lives.

Little by little, and one by one, the waves gently swallowed the tiny turtles. Once they were near the water, it was only a matter of waiting for a wave that would drag them inward. Each time we saw a wave take away one of these little reptiles, we knew it was on its way to reaching its destination. The small turtles that reached the sea had overcome a brief and important stage in their lives. Now another, more difficult one was awaiting them. In this last stage, we could no longer help them.

All we hotel guests—adults and children—had our sights and minds set on the two little turtles that we had gotten to place on the sand. What pleasure it was to see how they took their first steps and would stick out their little heads to see the few meters that they would cross over on the sand before getting into the water. Up above, the horizon began to show its reddish colors, as if it were blushing from the emotion of the spectacle there next to the sea, witnessing what was happening on the sand. Below, at the bottom of the sea, we would like to think that the mother and father turtles would gladly receive their offspring with joy. They, like us, would also be impatient for all the baby turtles to continue advancing on the sand in what was a welcome ceremony to life, which could well give us the illusion of being born again at a moment of sadness or nostalgia.

The Rainy Season

It had rained all day. The sun did not come out at all; the sky was covered by black clouds. The radio reported that a hurricane was coming, but that it would soon leave the area. Officials warned, however, that those who lived in coastal areas should not go out into the sea until everything calmed down. The next day, it continued to rain. It had not stopped during the whole night. The radio once again reported the weather, assuring us that the wind was dying down and that the danger would soon pass. The authorities recommended, however, that all vessels remain in port since accidents could still occur. The authorities also said they had sent help to those who were in danger.

The rain continued for three days and four nights. No one knew when it would stop because the radio had stopped transmitting its information about the weather, dedicating its time exclusively to broadcasting music. But on the sixth day, it once again mentioned the weather and stated that certain highways had been damaged. Therefore, the authorities recommended that residents not travel on these highways because there was a remote risk of accidents. The next day, buses and trucks stopped coming to the city, which then had no foodstuffs. It was thought that it was a precaution, and that things would return to normal. In a few days, the people thought, the trucks would come as always, full of foodstuffs and provisions of all types. But the trucks did not arrive, and the stored food was dwindling. The local authorities telegraphed the state ones, asking them why they hadn't sent food shipments. They answered that they should control the situation as much as possible because there were some problems, although not too important, with the rain. The people waited two days longer, listening to the music on the radio and looking for any news about the rain and any other problems it had caused that were unknown at the time. The weather report did not come, but in its place, there appeared old ads for various products. This made people forget a little about the scarcity of food and consume toothpaste, even if they didn't need it. Then, toothpaste became scarce, and, in its place, insecticides were placed on sale, which sold well due to the rain. The precipitation was still quite unyielding, causing plagues of unfamiliar insects that were highly destructive of wood and, particularly, of furniture.

A telegram was sent once again to the state authorities. This time, there was no response. Maybe the rain had broken the telegraph wires, making communication with the capital impossible. A call went out for volunteers to travel to the capital, but since everyone was combating plagues of mosquitos and other insects, no one went.

Two years after this happened, the inspectors and the state authorities arrived to investigate. They were all wearing raincoats and rubber boots. They estimated the extension of the city, the number of inhabitants that it had had, and several other aspects. They decreed that as soon as the rain stopped, they would bring settlers from the capital and other places, and that the city would be divided. They also announced that they would combat all plagues that made the place unhealthy. All of this would be done as soon as the rain stopped.

THE DESERT

I am the shadow of the desert, and I take on all visible forms during the day and night. I travel silently through the footpaths, pushed by the wind, and when I am close to the sea, the breeze refreshes me and drives me to continue on my way. I am a solitary squirrel who wanders through the desert paths. Also, if I so desire, I am a white bird with marvelous feathers who, without becoming agitated, sees strangers go by from afar. I, like you, am a rabbit resting in the shade of the thicket so that I will have the energy that will allow me to run untiringly among the cacti and dry shrubs. I am transformed, and I am a balmy view where the sea blends with the sand, and it looks like it is extending to the desert, to the bewilderment of the observer. Today, I decide to be an ancient olive tree that, during its entire life, has guarded an old church, and yesterday, I was an outcast who arrived at a place nonexistent on the maps of yore. In that reincarnation, I am an obstinate mountain with no top that is constantly chastised by the wind, whose fury hurls me toward the occult underground waterway that the palm follows faithfully and quietly. To my glory and arrogance, I am the best and most powerful carrion buzzard. I decide what small species lives or dies, and, without thinking about it or wanting to, I turn into an earth-filled road climbing through the mountains and leading to paths without end that, for many, have no return.

I discover myself in the reflection of a puddle of water that projects the image of an enormous rock painted in colors that tells a story and warns of the danger and perhaps of the possible death of a stranger. I am also the elongated cactus that stretches with zeal and an ardent desire to reach heaven one day. Don't expect too much of me. When the sea and I are together, and the oases are found in faraway places, the traveler gets desperate because neither of us two gives a drink to the thirsty.

In brief, I am an oasis of marvels that extends silently and eternally throughout the desert under the strong and stifling sunrays. Within me, I have drops of life to offer to some chosen ones or to those who know how to earn them. I am the past and the shade of the desert that extends through the horizon. I state it once again: from my entrails, there come, as an untiring woman in labor, squirrels, buzzards, birds with wondrous feathers, and hares that wander through the paths and hide under the thickets. Today, I can be the largest cactus that, without moving, watches the landscape; yesterday, I could have been a dry thicket at the bottom of a gorge that shelters and hides both a serpent and a rabbit, whatever chance or destiny imposes. Water flows through some of my ducts and concentrates in a life-or-death oasis. My precious liquid rests together with the millenary rocks that warn strangers of danger. I am also the dry roads full of sand and rocks that cause enormous clouds of dust, as the wind may want. Up above, the sun is watching me with fury, not letting up, and with fear that I might take pity on the beings that pass over my surface and break the millenary pact that we have of making them pay dearly with their lives to fools, the unwary, and the misguided.

I don't rest at night, either. When the moon shines on the firmament, small and large animals begin to come out silently from their lairs in search of food. Everything that moves becomes an appetizing and debatable spoil. Snakes, from their hideaways, watch and listen for whether the noise from the wind is altered or if something or someone is slowly coming near. Next to the road, on the rock, to one side of the gorge, or in any other place, other more cunning and more ravenous animals are hiding, such as large and majestic spiders and other starving carrion animals that are lying in ambush of the careless passerby.

Traveler, you are welcome. Be careful and move prudently. Watch that you don't wake the serpent up. And, for your good, I recommend that you be attentive to having no animal pick up your scent or follow your footprints or your tracks. Also, don't venture out on any road or footpath because they don't all lead to the destination that you are seeking or yearning for. Furthermore, some of these could lead you on a trip with no return; I warn you, the gorge is nearer and deeper than you think, and for the obstinate, it is synonymous with tragedy. If misfortune accompanies you and makes you fall, remember that this will be your end because, at the bottom of the gorge, death lies in wait for you. I hope it will be fast. Agony in the desert, it is said, is insufferable. Never perturb my tranquility. I watch everything day and night. I know everything, and I foretell everything, every movement, every thought, and all awkwardness. Due to this, I will see that you pay dearly for any carelessness, any irreverence, and, of course, any affront. Have no fear. I promise that when the moment comes, no one but me will dispose of your lifeless body. Destiny will make tragedy happen when, due to insignificant negligence, you lose your way for several days. The sun stupefies and confounds you so that you can pass away thirsty and desperate. Or it could happen when the sun, an honorable companion, decides to quickly undermine your senses and, in your desperation and unbearable pain, takes pity on you and, in the act of mercy, leads you to the gorge. The light, which is eternal, will blind you, and before you are disconcerted or lose your step and the way, everything will happen quickly.

After some time, the sun will begin to affect your skin. Further on, the dust and soil will first cover your face and then other parts of your body. The next stage is when the anxious and powerful buzzards will do what you and I know they irremediably must do. Never fear. I will never abandon you. You have nothing to repent of, perhaps only for your excessive trust in having mistaken one route with another, of awkwardly thinking that you would get to a certain place faster without consulting me first. Deep down, desert or sea, we will take you to the same destination. Up here is the buzzard that follows my orders. Down there, there are voracious fish that, under similar circumstances, will do the same. At the time of the agony, remember that an enormous cloud or wave will come to get you and shelter you. It doesn't matter if it is an enormous lie. As I said, never fear. I will always care for you and strive to help you reach your destination without delay.

72

AFRICAR

Toward the west, a mountain stands out. Those who know about this say that this is not about a hill like many others, but an active volcano known as the Popocatepetl, a little more than 5400 meters above sea level. Every day, the wind wanders through its exhalations of gas and ashes from every side. Some years ago, the expulsion from its throat or entrails was brutal. The cloud of volcanic dust traveled more than 70 kilometers toward the west and arrived in all parts of Mexico City. On TV and radio, they informed us that we had to sweep up the ashes and place them in trash bags. We should not throw water on them because the volcanic material hardens into cement with liquid.

On another occasion, the product of the exhalation of the volcano traveled toward the east. This time, the valley of Puebla was covered in ashes, and it was necessary to protect the animals that live in Africar, the place that is below the volcano. They said that none of the animals knew what was happening. For example, the Indian python saw from its enormous window that citizens were passing with rags to protect their faces from the ashes. Instead of snowflakes dropping, they were ashes. After a while, humans and animals became nervous. Luckily, as was proven the next day, nothing had happened. It seems that the animals were more intelligent and cautious than the humans. Wolves, hyenas, and black bears, among other species, were the first to look for refuge.

While the ashes were falling, all the animals kept silent. They had a feeling of foreboding and knew that something abnormal was happening. Maybe the crocodiles were the ones who feared the most. The darkness, odor, and silence of the other animals reminded them of when the sky was covered with dust thousands of years ago. The cloud that formed at that time was immense and took a long time to disappear. The animals and plants started to die little by little at that time. Fortunately, on this occasion, the same had not happened. The day after the ashes had fallen on Africar, the sun came out again. No one died, and everything began again in one great exhalation of volcanic material. Maybe, as some people thought, "Don Goyo," as the Popocatepetl is also known, was annoyed. The lesson was that nothing is written in stone. Therefore, today could be a misfortune, but tomorrow, perhaps, everything could be back to normal. The world, instead of ending, as it could have been foretold when the ashes began to fall, continued its course. This meant that evolution was not something to forget about, nor that the microorganisms had been the only living things to survive the episode when the dinosaurs were extinguished. Now, anything with a leg, wing, claw, feather, horn, or any other appendage or member on its body would preserve its current state. Nature, through the volcano, had only been inconvenienced momentarily.

The spider monkey, the suricates, and the flamingoes opined that perhaps, to be noticed from afar, the best thing the volcano could do would be to spit out all the madness and hate inside its poisoned entrails. Period. Thus, life would return to normality quickly. For these animals, personal problems are easy to solve. If anyone has any conflict that today is upsetting them, and is burning the soul and tomorrow the entrails, then the best that it can do is get it out, throw it as fire, be it with whomever, wherever. The longer one wants to keep up appearances, the cursed and unfortunate day will come around, and all that resentment and rancor will explode and destroy us inside. This happens to us, to Don Goyo, to a lion who went mad one day. In the case of the feline, it happens that he does not recall if his conduct was altered by jealousy, spite, or any other insult. In that terrible moment of ire and blindness, he attacked his female and killed her. At that instant, he didn't know anything. Still, the following day, he will begin to mourn the absence of his faithful companion. Days or weeks afterward, he may die of sadness when he forgets the tragic scene, looks for the dear companion of his life, and will not find her again. The idea that it has abandoned us forever, without our knowing or recalling, is what makes life lose its sense and appear to be now worth nothing. Oh! But things seemed quite easy at the moment of ire, violence, or total madness. In a moment of rage, life did not play fair with us. It did not want to warn us that we would be the first victims of our blunders.

For the animals who remember Mount Kilimanjaro, the sight of the Popocatepetl, the "Popo," as it is also known, is similar. Both are enormous mountains, proud of the important glacier at their top. If it weren't for global warming, the glacier would be larger than the one that is currently seen. It would shine in its entire splendor and look like a white handkerchief extended by a fine lady to cover her head from the penetrating sun the day she took a walk in the field. Giraffes, antelopes, and ostriches are perhaps the animals that most recall the joy of running freely in the proximity of Kilimanjaro. On the African plains, all those animals were passing by in total liberty. Their guardian and perpetual point of reference was Mt. Kilimanjaro. If some animals do not remember, it is because they have lost their memory. Others are already part of the new generation of beings that were born in Valsequillo on one side of the city of Puebla, near the pyramids of Cholula and Cacaxtla.

It has been more than 30 years since anyone imagined those savage beasts from Africa and other parts of the world would live and be born in proximity to the Popocatepetl!

Today, the animals in this new abode only see from afar the form of the Popo, but they cannot go near it. Deep down, this does not worry them. What causes them fear are the earthquakes, or when the land moves as if everything on the surface bothers it. The crocodile feels like someone that it can't see shakes off its body without authorization. Who is the daring one or the senseless one who does this? The giraffe, for its part, feels dizzy from its height. It has the sensation that it suddenly gets sick, and it is also sure that it will fall in the following seconds. In this alarming situation, the only thing that has worked for the crocodile before is raising its tail with fury and determination. This way, it lashes it down with fury onto the floor on both sides of its body. Thus, it tries to hide its fear when it doesn't know what is happening. With this punishment or this act of authority, the great reptile wants to tell the earth that it will hurt it as many times as necessary until it stops bothering it. The blows it gives with its tail are strong and come from someone who has decided to make itself understood and respected. What right does something that it can't see have (because it is invisible) to bother it?

In a short time, the earth stops moving. This probably happens because the amphibious tail-lashes hurt part of the surface of the earth. However, throughout the earthquake, the giraffe thought that its dizziness would never stop and that its health would worsen irremediably if the crazy movement in its legs continued. Instinctively, it extended its four extremities as much as it could. Then, it lowered its neck and tried to maintain its precarious equilibrium and the hope that everything was a fleeting nightmare. The relief that it felt was enormous when the earth stopped moving. It swore that it would never enter a bar or drink alcohol excessively.

The ostrich was walking at that time, and it wanted to know where the stupid movement was coming from that didn't allow it to walk at its pleasure. As always, it hid its head in a hole to try to see what was happening below. Since its eyes took time to get used to the darkness, it didn't see anything. When it took its head out of that hole to ask what had happened, everything had calmed down, as if by magic. This bird, which runs at great speed, will never understand what has happened. Deep down, it doesn't worry much about knowing the technical details of what an earthquake is or how it is produced. Life has taught it that it cannot fling itself, pecking furiously to fight against something invisible and unknown.

The earthquake made the Indian python roll up as much as possible its more than three meters long. The beautiful scales of green and brown color of its body become hard and indicate that something important is happening to it or bothering it. Like other animals, it feels offended by the uncontrolled and undesired movement of its body. It is possible that someone is making a joke in bad taste or that an elephant has attacked it by raising its trunk and wants to throw it against the rocks. Since eternity is eternity, and the world is the world, elephants and pythons have hated each other. Both animals have shared the same geography and have not learned to coexist. The python knows that the only way to beat the elephant is to wrap itself around its neck and strangle it with all the force of its muscles. The elephant, for its part, knows that it can defeat the python if it steps on it multiple times until it breaks it into many pieces. Or it can pick it up with its trunk and throw it with brutal force into the void, where it will eventually smash onto enormous and merciless rocks.

On this occasion, something different is happening that moves the python. The elephant is absent, which is why something more powerful than that pachyderm, and which merits respect, has rocked the python against its will. During the seconds in which that powerful and invisible being shook it, the reptile experienced an unexplainable change in personality. It felt several times that it could be free again if it threw itself against the crystal, which was limiting its dwelling and distancing it from the exterior world. Thus, it would conquer its liberty again. It would begin to charge invoices and show its enormous power to any living thing before it. It would also stop being an observer, or a passive being, and become an active one. Now, it would feel like an important actor who could dominate the place. Everything would be under its control. The Indian python would again rule and decide who lives and who should be gobbled up.

The energy and vitality that the python feels make it think about the possibility of not being the curiosity of the passersby. Instinctively, that is what it has always tried to do, since it has a memory. Today, for example, if anyone stops in front of its large window, the python doesn't stop feeling curiosity. Its nature tells it to inspect the boy, the old man, or the adult who stops at a little more than a meter's distance. Every time it sees someone in front of its window, it recalls its ancestry's grandeur. Then it becomes attentive to the possible victim, the great piece of food, or the living trophy that fears it. Meanwhile, its head goes up and down agilely, supported and boosted by the rest of its body. Thus, it carefully measures and studies a possible victim or a probable adversary, and it is beginning to yearn for its grandiose past when it was hanging, mistaken for the large branches of the trees, attentive to everything around it.

Previously, when it was free, this exercise was the antecedent of the quick movement it would use to gobble up the victim. Today, the eyes of the python are sad. It would wish to swallow any spectator, not due to hunger or wickedness, but only for the wish to be the respected and feared reptile that it once was. If it were free, it would drag at full speed on the ground, through the valley of Puebla, through the streets, and arrive at the center of the city of Puebla. Once there, it could go to the pyramids of Cholula and Cacaxtla. All would try to flee from the enormous animal that they considered to be the modern reincarnation of Quetzalcoatl, an enormous and strange snake. It would behave with the expected fierceness of that pre-Hispanic deity. It would attack all men and other living beings that it had within its reach, only to meet the required sacrifice so that all things in the world could continue to function normally.

The wish of the python to be free once again is very intense. But greater is the frustration when it realizes, again, that between its impulse and its refinding of liberty, there is a transparent barrier that it wants to destroy, although it cannot, nor even knows how to do it. This obstacle hurts its self-esteem. It does not feel like a great python or a great wonder animal of nature. Its misfortune is the same as that of any worm of the earth that doesn't have time to hide in its hole before someone, without realizing it, squashes it with a horrible and insensitive old shoe.

The python dreams. Something tells it that many memories give it an enormous impulse to free itself from captivity. The memories revive the desire to return to the place in the world that saw its birth—there, far away in India. Those wishes or impulses are forthcoming from something unknown. An instinct tells it that there, in America, a python is a very powerful being—one that the mortals of the past would have adored and considered an invincible god. It only needed some of its scales to become feathers for it to turn into a sacred feathered serpent. Not far away, in Cacaxtla, in the fine mural paintings of that pre-Hispanic place, is the vision of what the great reptile or marvelous serpent could come to be, showing that it transports the Olmecan Xicalangan priest by land, and why not, through the heavens. Today, it would be a serpent at the foot of the stairs of the pyramid on which human sacrifice would take place. Its function would be essential to preserving the world's equilibrium. It only needed to be there, where the pyramid begins, to gobble up the one to be sacrificed, already lifeless. The python would become a powerful Quetzalcoatl of flesh, blood, and scales, and the one brought from heaven with the light and force of lightning to be present when ordering and directing the world. The Indian python and the benign feathered serpent would be immortal if they only knew how to have two heads, change some scales for feathers, and bring themselves down from heaven in the form of lightning to be present in all places. Thus, they would win the unconditional respect of humans and animals.

The hippopotamuses, for their part, do not worry about what is happening. They think that if the earth sustains their weight, then the earth is good; it is noble, something they must venerate. They also think that they can be indebted permanently to the earth, being that each time they walk, it thunders slightly. They also know that the best they can do when there is an earthquake is lie down on the ground. Experience tells them that even though many calamities happen, they never affect an animal of their size. They only ask for a little bit of food, some water to humidify their dry skin, and a comfortable place on the ground to lie down and rest at the end of the day, without any worry. Who, deep down, has different wishes from those of the hippopotamuses?

In Africar, there is a great diversity of monkeys. If these animals are usually nervous and restless by nature, the thing that makes them worse is an earthquake. They yell and move from place to place, pushing each other and having an attack of collective hysteria. Given this deplorable conduct, no one would like to be reincarnated as a monkey. Maybe some would prefer to return to this world in the form of an orangutan with the intent of helping their neighbors be free of lice and other bugs.

The female papion, for its part, knows that the offspring should be taken care of and protected. For this reason, they should be safeguarded, hugging them with strength and fear close to their stomachs. The male is conscious that it should always be close to its offspring. The other monkeys prefer to climb trees. They have the idea that if the earth opens up, it will first swallow other animals and then the trees. The monkeys can escape that tragic end. Maybe they'll do it by jumping from one tree to another and will perish only if the earth has swallowed up all the world's vegetation and the only thing left is an enormous hole. Few know this, but from this cavity, a million bats will come flying out in the full light of day to fly in circles over and over again, trying to be oriented in a world that is cracking. The ashes from the Popo may be the first sign of these events; that is, the ash rain that the volcano is spitting out will precede the earthquake. At the moment the Earth decides to open up everywhere, for the world to end, it will finish being eaten up by its lava.

It is known that with the breaking of the Earth's crust, the last and largest of all calamities will be released. Bats, which are also considered flying mice full of fury and rabies, will seek food that no longer exists. On their way, they will ravish all living beings. It is also possible that they will seek their brothers living in a false cavern of Africar and try to free them. Flying mice, free and captive, will only come in contact with the howling that they make and from the noise of their innumerable wings, being that the glass that divides them resists everything, even the strongest and most startling earthquake that can exist. The only act of solidarity among these nocturnal mammals will be to hang themselves from the ceiling, walk along the walls of the cave, nail down the claws of their extremities, and issue sound after sound, seeking a location, a point of reference. And, since they will be unable to set up direct contact with their captive brothers, the best they can do is join one another and return flying to the place of departure. Thus, they will enter the large caverns that take them to the center of the Earth, to the place where all rocks walk because they are liquid, and also everything petrifies gradually. The last thing one hears in this place is the penetrating and frightening screeching of the innumerable groups of bats, which, before a useless world, decide to sacrifice themselves by letting themselves drop to the ground on liquid rocks that are boiling at very high temperatures.

The earthquake enlivens the hyenas. Anything that looks like a calamity or bad luck causes them delight and joy. For them, the quake is an opportunity to be present in the pain and tragedy of their neighbors. Perhaps the movement of the ground makes some animals die little by little, which gets their morale up. Between their mocking laughter and their longing for destruction, they will escape from where they are confined. They will run all over to make an accounting of the damage and the dead. If they could speak, they would say, "We are gravediggers. We live off the morgue." Better yet, they should say, "We are the morgue, and we have come to get you." They are not interested in being more precise, and they think that no animal should escape them alive, no matter how large it is. They look at the elephant, and they know that someday, they, or their descendants will savor those marvelous and gigantic bones. It doesn't matter where the pachyderm is buried. Part of the happiness and joy of being a hyena consists of knowing how to exhume all dead bodies and do whatever they like with them. Elephants, camels, vicunas, and all other inhabitants of the Africar, when they die, will be succulent and marvelous dishes for the restless and insatiable fangs of the hyenas. They only must be patient and then receive (why not?) help from a strong earthquake to alter the rhythm of their monotonous lives. If the animals don't die due to a determined cause, the hyenas can help them get to eternal peace. Only a visionary is necessary to free them from the place where they are captive, and they, gratefully, take charge of the rest.

The great deception that the hyenas suffer is that the earthquake wasn't long and didn't have sufficient intensity to knock trees down. Therefore, it didn't cause lamentable accidents where one or more lives could be lost. Damn it! The earthquake comes, which promises emotion and food, and then ends in frustrating peace, where the services of a gravedigger are not required. Instead of having generated the expected misfortune, the earth's movement was like a delicate and spontaneous lulling of a cradle. This had happened before, but the hyenas, so it is said here and there, are dreamers, and they get false expectations from everything because they can't contain their desire to smell death. In effect, the earthquake ends and the hyenas, as always, go back to sleep on the ground, and they again dream of attacking in a group this or that animal that has separated from its flock. It is said that a hyena has nightmares, and that it is on the verge of a nervous breakdown when it dreams that it is alone and knows it must fight for its life against another savage animal of its size. Today, they are not seen as nervous; they are only disappointed about life. On this occasion, the misfortune for them was that there was no misfortune. Instead of laughing, some say that they can be heard lamenting their cursed luck.

At several dozen meters from the hyenas, the robust American bison are walking around. The earth's movement makes them think that soon there will be a great flock of their companions. Instinctively, all the bison get ready to join this great race, both psychically and psychologically. They want to join that flock of companions to return to the Great Plains of the United States. They know that they will first have to go out of Puebla and then go toward Hidalgo; then, they will rectify their course toward Queretaro. Thereinafter, everything is like singing, since they will be going straight to the north. After Queretaro comes San Luis Potosi, and then Nuevo Leon. At the time when they least expect it, they will run and snort on Texas soil. All the cowboys of the region will be surprised and fascinated by the spectacle that would have been the envy of Buffalo Bill. Since the middle of the nineteenth century, no similar flock had been seen of such great attractiveness, so full of energy, or whose numerous members ran with so much joy. If the earth trembled like in the old times, then the remaining Sioux and Apache souls would want to go out hunting with their old bows and arrows, riding their obedient pinto horses bareback, while all the American bison of Africar would direct the flock by turns and at great speed.

The earth movement says it is a thing of a few seconds, so the Africar bison may tell the flock leader to pick them up. Meanwhile, the bison dream for an instant. They think that once they are on U.S. soil, they will run on the prairies of that country like their ancestors did. They will be free again and on their feet. Their joy will be reborn from the speedy race, and the enormous dust storm will be left behind. The range will go from Texas to southern Canada. There, the difference from other places is that there are no wakes on the sea, but the dream of an American bison that lives in Africar, stands firmly and with force on the rocky path and recognizes itself as free, full of energy and vitality. This quadruped wants to take its enormous body where the steep and rocky slopes and roads are such that the strong and cold wind that blows from the mountains will hit it right on its face, will comfort it, and encourage it on the journey. In this way, it feels good to be alive and free.

Maybe on another occasion, the American bison of the Africar will manage to materialize their desires for liberty because some time ago, the earth stopped moving, and the great stock of companions that were waiting didn't go by to pick them up. Oh! How sad! If they don't come for them, these animals won't find a way to return home, and their species will continue to be in constant danger of extinction. "Something has to be done," they tell each other. "Everything except losing hope," answers the strongest and most experienced bison of Africar. He knows what he is talking about. When he got to this place, he was sad and lonely. Then, over the years, other companions arrived, and later, some of its species were born inside the park.

At that moment, the mother bison did not agree to abandon Africar. In no other place in the world will they be as respected as here. No male of their species contradicts them. No one wants fights or family problems, least of all with their wives. The only ones that don't understand are the young bison who don't have a partner and opt to pant and walk between the cars that wait to see them. They get away a little from the cars and seek a piece of ground where they can wipe their feet with sadness, nostalgia, and force. They haven't realized it, but among all of them, they draw a map of the great American plains that someday, thanks to their yearning for liberty, they will run upon full of energy and joy. Boy! Who could be an American bison! The flock could go from Canada down to Tierra del Fuego, if the Darien Gap didn't exist, in just a few days. Its members would invite the moose, vicunas, and capybaras so they might join them in their long escapade. They only need the desire and the will to start the march at full speed and for the wind to blow with strength so that every time their feet thunder on the ground, they feel like the wind is caressing their faces and making them grunt with joy.

The king of the jungle yawned. He must ensure that his felines conduct themselves as they should and that the young lions are not going around creating problems. He also must make sure that everything works in an optimal way because he knows that his leadership (all lions are leaders by nature) must be transmitted to all the other animals in the place where he lives. If there is an emergency in the area, who, except for him, will resolve the problem? If the owners of the place had a little modern business vision, they would have named the lion the general manager. By so doing, the equilibrium among the species would be guaranteed, and the lion's authority would be explicit. Even though one can sometimes complain about the food and installations in Africar, it is necessary to have someone with well-worn trousers to keep things in order, growling, and warning about punishment for those who don't respect orders and who do not allow others to live in peace. In what other way would the other animals be warned that they must stop grumbling and fighting at late hours so that there will be peace, and everyone can sleep their required eight hours daily?

Okay. This or that species slept well. There is no problem there, but now comes the tedious part. No one thinks it's funny to see the unceasing automobile pilgrimage all day every day. There comes a time when everyone gets tired, and the species are at the point of dying of boredom. One earthquake now creates disorder, and its happenings serve to change the routine a little and make staying in the place more pleasant. If the decisions were in his claws, the lion would do two things: first, he would name an animal commission to investigate what was happening in the Popocatepetl. No one has died from the fumaroles that the volcano is spitting out into the atmosphere. But why wait until misfortune presents itself? In the second place, he would name another commission to evaluate the effects of the earthquake that had just happened. At the moment, he had the intuition that nothing happened, but he did hear that the monkeys overreacted to the events, in addition to the fact that other species were worked up to a great measure. He thinks that so much commotion, even though it is due to nothing, always disturbs everyone.

In the commissions he forms, he will abstain from including any hyenas. He knows that they have always been famous for being hypocritical and treacherous in fights. In the past, when he had them close, he didn't turn its back on them. However, now he thinks that it is best to keep them far away and never give them responsibilities. Maybe it would be most convenient to have a known and charismatic elephant be head of the commission that is going to inspect the Popo and a black bear to take charge of making an accounting of the quake. The idea is to know objectively what happens inside their home and its surroundings. In this sense, the good judgment of the elephant and the precautions that the bear takes are the best recommendation cards for each of them to take those positions.

Before the lion considers another relevant matter of Africar, he will review all the members of his species with his eyes. He has the nine felines, as always. He expects that the demographic explosion will soon moderate. He wants to ask the watchmen whether there is any novelty. He knows that it is a useless bother, since the caretakers are much more worried about how the quake could have affected their families and their homes than about performing their duties well in the workplace. Under those conditions, you cannot get very far, he tells himself, and he prefers to take things with a little philosophy. He throws himself on the ground again. He doesn't know what happened, but instead of yawning from laziness and tiredness, as always, this time a strong unplanned roar comes out of his mouth, disquieting all the animals there. Before the powerful king of the jungle knows anything more, he decides to rest from his daily worries. If it weren't for him, who else would worry so that things go well in Africar?

The lion rests and begins to dream that he is not in Puebla, but close to Kilimanjaro. He only wants to go out sometimes to get food. In the dream, he sees himself getting far from the mountain and encouraging himself to go hunting and chase intelligent animals of great size. He doesn't like the first part of this scene. Internally, he feels that he is evading his responsibilities by getting far from the mountain. While asleep, he slaps his paws in the air as a sign of disapproval of his conduct. In the dream, he starts his way back. Now, little by little, Kilimanjaro has been transformed into the Popo. Something tells him internally that he belongs to the new generation of animals that were born in Africar. If one day he visits Kilimanjaro, he knows he will feel a certain emotion when seeing numerous animals, although emotionally he won't feel the same if, instead of unknowns, it would be about animals with which he has lived all its life. Between Popocatepetl and Kilimanjaro, he doesn't doubt and chooses the Popo. He is used to the ash exhalations that the volcano spits out with force, and that sometimes he can see from the high part of his den. If the Popo is all right, he thinks, everything is all right. Also, there is nothing like one's home. Who knows what bad habits and tricks the animals that live and roam close to

Kilimanjaro are full of? Here, in this place that is close to the Popo, everyone knows everyone. It is well known who to trust and who not to trust. Also, who would know how difficult life would be in that part of Africa? Here in Puebla, everything is simple and foreseeable. If there is a dry spell, no one cares because no one is affected; food and water arrive every day at the hours set. Maybe all of this has to do with the Popo.

Therefore, he is the king of the jungle and, consequently, also of Africar. His place is at the head here. He will roar with all the force that his lungs and vocal cords permit each time he wants to be heard by all the animals. Although sometimes it seems that he is resting, and that he is dozing off, he is always aware of everything. That is why he came back quickly from his dream of Kilimanjaro to stay at the head of his obligations. Once he is convinced that he has made the best decision, he will open his eyes. At that moment, they were filled with the fabulous spectacle of an enormous and potent exhalation of volcanic material from the Popo.

One day, the lion will roar in the same way, and with the same force that the volcano exhales ashes. His powerful roar will not only come to calm down Don Goyo's spirits, but it will go much further. First, it will arrive in Veracruz, and from there, it will depart, boosted by the strong wind and high waves, up to Africa. All the animals near Puebla and those living on that faraway continent will know about the joy he transmits by knowing and, what's more, feeling that he is the king of the jungle and Africar. He knows that when that unrestrained and powerful roar will surge it will be heard in Kilimanjaro and its surroundings. Thus, it will greet all the animals of that distant and fascinating place. It will also let them know that here, on the hillside of the Popo, there is joy and a new generation of savage animals that love the place where they live.

Beast, Master, and Tambourine

What's my name? I don't remember. I think that at some time in my life, I had amnesia, and I was left without a past and with a present that I still can't understand. I don't know where it will take me. I have heard that sometimes my master calls me Strong Rock, Powerful Fur, and Magic Bear from Durango. This last is the nickname that I most like because I feel that it genuinely describes that I'm an elderly thin bear with parched skin and done in. I live, like many others, in Mexico City. Perhaps in my youth, I belonged to a circus where I possibly got sick and, in one careless moment of misfortune, which I know nothing about, lost my memory. Due to this, I am not going from city to city dressed elegantly, riding a bicycle, or making jests better than any unenthusiastic clown could do. Thus, to the extent that I am not linked by work to a prestigious circus, I must recognize that I earn my living by making public presentations. Although somewhat modest, they are still based on hard work, on one hand, and routine, on the other, considering the misfortune of being an old crock for modern society.

I have said that I think I suffer from amnesia because I remember little about my life. That's the way it is. My memory covers only this period of my existence. I have known only two bitter things: extenuating work—repaid in what is essential and without any consideration—and solitude. This last is the worst punishment that anyone can imagine. We have all felt it at one time or another in our lives. Maybe the adolescent who fled from his parents because they did not understand him, or the boy whose friends always made fun of and humiliated him, know exactly what I'm referring to. In my case, the minimum elements, like some affection, a word of encouragement, or worthy treatment, are not present in my life these days. This lonely life never ends; it repeats itself day after day, giving me no respite. No child will come to play with me because my master always has me confined. Neither is there an old person who will stealthily pet me when he passes by me, distracted. There is no affection or consideration of any kind toward me.

Maybe before I got amnesia, life was kinder to me, possibly a little more benign. Perhaps I had a sweetheart or a family who cared about me before. Now, I have no one except for a cage where I spend most of the day enslaved and an intolerant and irascible master who only seeks excuses to hit me and hurt me with his whip. He gets me out of the cage, where he has me confined to train me or go out to the street. Before I get out of the cell, he puts a muzzle on me, if he ever took it off. Cursed be the contrivance! I would like to put it on him when he is thirsty or when his stomach hurts from hunger, and he can't even eat if the food is within reach! He never lets me be without chains. He is not dumb, and he knows how to place them on me and entangle them around my body so that my muscles have no strength, and he can control me easily. So despicable and useless is the life that I live!

Usually, my master lets me out in the mornings to train me. In the beginning, he played the tambourine, and with lashes from his whip, he forced me to move at the rate of the tambourine as I was dancing. Many times, I grumbled in rage. On various occasions, I wanted, with all my fury, to put an end to this heartlessness. But I could not. I was impeded by the chains and the muzzle. Also, he always properly protected himself from any unnecessary or uncontrolled risks that he might have had with me. Every time I grumbled, I felt the lashes from his whip on my body, one after the other. They weren't just one or two; they were always many and excessive. I don't know when this was, but on one occasion in which he felt that I was cross and maybe a little violent, he hit me with the most extreme harshness and coldness that one can imagine. The punishment and pain were enormous. From various parts of my skin, there sprouted blood and intense pain. At first, I felt more fury and then tremendous frustration because I couldn't defend myself. That was when his blows began to break my mood and force me to give in totally and forever quit my various intents at rebelliousness.

My master never gave me anything in exchange for my obedience. Little by little, his mistreatment eroded me internally. He made me desire to be free so I could disappear. He also made me consider myself a foolish, fearful animal without the necessary courage to end a miserable, senseless life. How was it possible that I, a bear with brown fur, could be humiliated and mistreated this way? Maybe this happened because I endured a more significant dose of punishment than any other could have taken before dying. Or perhaps because one of those whippings hit me with a good sound blow straight where I had kept my pride and my self-esteem and destroyed them forever. Maybe the reason is that my life is truly miserable and lonely. Since I can remember, I have known nothing but mistreatment and humiliation. And I have accepted them by the force of punishment and need, maybe because my conservation instinct is profound and my pride very weak. This reality has fractured my dignity.

Today, as on many other days, I went out with my master. He was taking me through the street, chained, and with the muzzle on. The two of us were walking on the sidewalk, and when someone saw us from afar, that person would change from that side of the street or take refuge in his home. We scared many people. For them to see that they should not fear me, my master showed his strength. He would pull the chain with overwhelming force and give me several lashes. Frankly, these blows didn't hurt me because my master hit me as part of the show rather than as punishment. He also knew that if he hit me excessively, he would risk hurting me and making it hard for him to take me home, especially if I injured a leg or dropped on the asphalt exhausted and became unable to walk.

One day, I felt a fire burning on my back. His whip fell with force on my backbone many times. My reaction to this intense pain made me get up on two legs and then fall flat on my face. I could not move for a long time, not just one or two hours. I lost consciousness in this lapse. I recall that my master was worried about his lifestyle being over forever. When I regained consciousness,

I thought that my master was wretched. "This dumb one doesn't realize that he is clumsier and more inhumane than I," I thought. I believe that, but for my dignity, I should have died.

As I have said, and we have done many times since the Vertiz Narvarte section began to fill with people, my master and I walk down Vertiz Avenue. Along this street, we will give four, or if there are many people, up to seven presentations before lunch. So, I must walk at his rate. First, as always, the chains are taut to reduce my movement and response capacity, and then he punishes me.

"Stupid animal! Don't you know that I am the only one in charge here?" he would yell at me, and as always, he would do it every time he started to hit me. I know I shouldn't grumble because I will suffer more severely if I do. I must drop to the ground and let him give vent to his fury and make him think that I have repented of my doing. Once he considers that the lesson is sufficient and that I have shown that I understood what he wanted to tell me, my master loosens the chain and pulls it up to indicate that I must get up and continue walking.

The experience indicates to me that my master has measured his blows. He knows when to hit with rage to hurt and when only to reprimand at the appropriate time so that the possible discrepancy between him and me doesn't go unnoticed. I know that he doesn't want to kill me because I'm his only source of income. He had tolerated me in this activity all these years, just because he would have had economic problems without me. Due to this, he provides me with minimum food. He demands rudely that I learn his movements and dance routines. If I get sick, he cures me only because he worries that his source of income doesn't disappear. What would he do without me? Who would he punish with his whip? Who would he chain and almost drag down the city's streets from his family? Who would he make responsible for his fury and frustration? To whom would he say that he was born with a whip in his hand, and that he would die with that punishment object between his fingers and that no one would take it from his hands? I believe that his wife and two children are grateful that I exist. Because the fear, which from far I can guess is in their eyes, tells me that they feel that my master won't attack them if I'm at his disposition. The expression on those three faces reveals that each of them thinks that if my master were to deal blows with his whip on any of them, it would be easy for him to extend its impact on his other two loved ones. None of them would be safe from his whip and the blindness in his brain. Who of my master's family will let themselves be hit with fury today and always, without asking at the climactic moment, for vengeance in return?

There are days and situations, I don't know, that this can only be perceived under certain circumstances when I think that my days are counted. I don't know when I'll die, but I have seen how the two persons, who are in the Animal Control van, have rebuked my master in a hostile way. First, they ask him if there is any proof that I have been given all the necessary vaccines that an animal of my species requires. Then they ask him to show them the permit to own a bear and to walk it around as if nothing, like any other mascot, through the city streets. My master smiles. He doesn't answer. He puts his hand in the pocket of his old pants to get the bill he has always prepared for these situations. He pulls it out and extends it to them in silence. The Animal Control people take the money, and they tell him that next time, they'll be more severe, and they get into their van, and slam the door hard so that everyone hears it and knows who the authority is. Then, like yesterday and always, the Animal Control van takes off in the opposite direction to ours. My master waits for that vehicle to go away. After a while, when it has finally disappeared, he begins to yell several times furiously: "Sons of bitches, muck bureaucrats!", and he raises his arm like he would want to curse the Animal Control persons for life.

The following week, or when one least expects it, he will find them again, repeating the story. Once again, there will be threats to show that they are tough, and maybe one will feel like checking whether my chains and muzzle are adequate. It is easy to suppose that, deep down, what they want to do is to get me up on their van, although they won't dare do it because they fear I will become furious, destroy something, and escape. Maybe this is what worries them the most, being they are second-class bureaucrats, that anything makes them corrupt, and they always run away from any indication of anything that might commit them. I know if they got me on their van, they wouldn't take me to the Animal Control offices to confine me in one of their cages. They wouldn't either call the zoo for them to take charge of me and give me a better life. They would deviate from their route and go to some place where they could sell me or, better for them, kill me, peel my fur off, and have a coat of their dreams made. For them, alive or dead, I am worth a lot of money. Even though they are unsure when they will get me up on their van and take me where I won't cause them any problems, I won't escape, I can keep living peacefully. When this situation changes, my days are counted. It is possible that, at that moment, the Animal Control van represents the best option that I have for ending my existence with dignity.

When my master and I get to a corner that he likes and that seems adequate to him, he begins to play the tambourine to call the people's attention.

"Come and see the great savage bear from Durango that has been tamed for you," he begins to tell them in a loud and professional tone.

As part of the beginning of the spectacle, I get up several times, and I introduce myself to two legs so that all who are there can see me clearly.

"Come and see how 'The Great Bear from Durango' dances. Come and get close to enjoy a family event," my master repeats, full of enthusiasm and with an advertising emphasis.

The event doesn't start until a considerable number of people are gathered around us. Then, when he estimates that the people who join will provide an attractive tip, the event begins. He introduces me again. He tells them that he trapped me on the mountain range, "Around there, where Pancho Villa did his bit between Chihuahua and Durango." He also tells the public that one day he feared for his life, being that I attacked him while he slept and almost yanked off one of his arms. However, he never uncovers this extremity or shows it to the public, so they may see any scar, which is why I think he is lying.

My acting begins formally when my master plays the tambourine for almost a half-minute. This is my call to the stage and the warning that the whole spectacle must result to his heart's content. Then he starts to sing, and when he hits the ground with the whip, I get up on two legs and begin to dance. I am attentive to my master's voice, his movements, and the instrument's sound because, that way, I know what I must do. Sometimes I dance in circles and others back and forth in small steps. I know that I must dance only three pieces, not one more. In the last one, I dance standing up, and he comes near me and hugs me from afar, and the two of us dance and move our feet in certain coordination as if we were beloved comrades on our way through this life. Finally, he leans his head on one side of my body and says out loud so everyone can hear, "My friend, take care of me while I sleep."

Then my master pretends to be snoring, and I pretend to rock him and lull him to sleep with my back. The muzzle, the chains, and the position he is in impede me from doing any damage to him. This is the act that most surprises me and calls the people's attention and why the people give us part of their money gladly.

A few seconds after the people applauded, my master withdraws from me. He takes one step back and turns on his heel. He then tells our spectators, "Friends, allow me to call your attention for a few coins for Strong Rock's food. A few coins, so Strong Rock can continue to dance." My master just finishes, saying these words, and immediately, he tries to establish visual contact with those present to incite them in this way to provide a good tip. For my part, I must remain on two legs for a while, drop to the four legs, and turn in small semi-circles to get up once again on two legs.

Tomorrow, or a day after tomorrow, in the presentation corresponding to that day, my master will change my name and say that my name is Powerful Fur. If he is in a good mood, he will refer to me as the Magic Bear from Durango.

One day, I was in the middle of a spectacle, dancing on two legs when, suddenly, I felt a strong annoyance and great pain in the lower part of my back. Someone, maybe an aggressive or unpleasant spectator, attacked me with something sharp and laughed at me. Instinctively, I grunted loudly and, as I would have never done before on the stage, I turned quickly and gave several slaps in the air. I still had time to grumble some more toward the spectators and make clear part of my aggressiveness and the change in my mood.

Something was telling me not to accept that aggression, because I was doing well in the part of the act that corresponded to me. Also, I was offended that this was about a punishment that was coming from a member of the public and not from my master. The worst came a little later. My master became infuriated with me. He didn't like for me to grumble in public and much less that I swing my arms aggressively in front of our spectators. The event ended. Now, the situation was something else because, in his mind, there was a mad bear out of control that could attack the public, our clientele, to make the master lose the money that those assisting at the presentation would have given us happily.

A little after my abrupt action, how my master pulled me full of hate and ire! The violent tug of the main chain that held me went to one side for me to lose control. I fell to the ground, defenseless. Before I could realize it, my master was hitting me savagely and insistently with his whip. Over and over again, as he had never done before. He was out of himself. He didn't want to see that I would have never done any damage to anyone with those chains on me.

"Damn you!" My master yelled at me several times. He was beside himself and continued to hit me unceasingly on the most sensitive parts of my extremities and my backbone, and on the other places where he knew the pain would be excessive. I learned my miserable lesson. I also learned that this punishment would not only be extreme and senseless mistreatment, but also the only warning that he would give me in life. Now, before starting to work and dance, I start moving softly from one side to another without bothering my master. Also, to indicate that the people should keep their distance. That is, for their own good, to remain far from the bear in movement. If I could talk, I would tell all the spectators who came near me, if I didn't beg them, to show them my scars, to please remain behind an imaginary line, because I need that space to work without errors and not hurt anyone. In this way, I think I will avoid the last and most severe punishment that my master will gladly give me. The next time my master punishes me, I know he will pull the main chain from the part of the neck with great force and with no mercy. He will teach me, the clumsy bear that I am, that I only have one master and that even if it is the last thing he will do, my useless destiny is to obey him always.

95